Con

Spear Books

Sugar Daddy's Lover Rosemarie Owino
Lover in the Sky Sam Kahiga
A Girl Cannot Go on Laughing All the Time Magaga Alot
The Love Root Mwangi Ruheni
The Ivory Merchant Mwangi Gicheru
A Brief Assignment Ayub Ndii
A Taste of Business Aubrey Kalitera
No Strings Attached Yusuf K. Dawood
A Woman Reborn Koigi wa Wamwere
The Bhang Syndicate Frank Saisi
My Life in Crime John Kiriamiti
Black Gold of Chepkube Wamugunda Geteria
Ben Kamba 009 in Operation DXT David Maillu
Son of Woman Charles Mangua
A Tail in the Mouth Charles Mangua
The Ayah David Maillu
A Worm in the Head Charles K. Githae
Twilight Woman Thomas Akare
Life and Times of a Bank Robber John Kiggia Kimani
Son of Woman in Mombasa Charles Mangua
My Life with a Criminal: Milly's Story John Kiriamiti
The Operator Chris Mwangi
Three Days on the Cross Wahome Mutahi
Birds of Kamiti Benjamin Bundeh
Nice People Wamugunda Gateria
Times Beyond Omondi Mak'Oloo
Lady in Chains Genga-Idowu
Mayor in Prison Karuga Wandai
Son of Fate John Kiriamiti
Kanina and I Charles Mangua
Prison is not a Holiday Camp John Kiggia Kimani
Confessions of an AIDS Victim Carolyne Adalla
Comrade Inmate Charles K. Githae
Colour of Carnations Ayub Ndii
The American Standard Sam DeSanto
From Home Guard to Mau Mau Elisha Mbabu
The Girl was Mine David Karanja
Links of a Chain Monica Genya
Unmarried Wife Sitwala Imenda
Dar es Salaam By Night Ben Mtobwa
The Sinister Trophy John Kiriamiti
Kenyatta's Jiggers Charles Mangua
A Place of No Return Mervil Powell

Confessions of an AIDS Victim

Carolyne Adalla

Spear Books
NAIROBI • KAMPALA • DAR ES SALAAM

Published by Spear Books
a subsidiary of
East African Educational Publishers Ltd.
Brick Court, Mpaka Road/Woodvale Grove
Westlands, P.O. Box 45314, Nairobi

East African Educational Publishers Ltd.
P.O Box 11542, Kampala

Ujuzi Educational Publishers Ltd
P.O. Box 31647, Kijito-Nyama, Dar es Salaam

First published 1993

Reprinted 1999, 2002

ISBN 9966-46-846-3

Typeset by Jarodi Educational Institute, Nairobi

Printed in Kenya by English Press Ltd.
Enterprise Road, P.O. Box 30127, Nairobi

For Valery Charity Atieno
– It is a world you must live in

and

For the Spitzer family in the Netherlands
– You are too good to be forgotten

Chapter One

Dear Marilyn,

By the time this letter gets to you, several weeks, months or years may have passed by, so I will not start with the usual greetings. Writing it beats all purpose and reason, but am I left with any other way in which I can express my grief and share my thoughts without affecting my life? Indeed, writing proves to be the only way I can emotionally vent my feelings and probably the feelings of many others in a similarly awkward position, for mine is a human tragedy. It has shaken me to the core of my heart and even as I write, I am visibly trembling.

'It is not possible; it is not true.' I have said these words over and over during the past three days. It is like a dream from which I hope to be shaken awake and realise that after all, it isn't true.

'What are you talking about, Cathy?' I can hear you ask soberly.

Without creating much suspense on your part, I will be very candid with the facts. In your last letter you asked me how far I had gone with my plans of travelling to Texas for my second degree. Considering the length of time it will take this letter to reach you, you may be easily mistaken in thinking that I did succeed in such plans and conveniently forgot to maintain the communication link between us. Worse still, you might fear that I died in a plane crash or something like that. That is far from the reality.

Now, you know from your own experience that before a student travels abroad these days, his blood is tested as part of the immigration requirements. It was after receiving the results of this test, three days ago, that I was told I am seropositive. This, I am informed, is a condition in which antibodies to a particular organism are found in the blood. It indicates that the individual has been exposed to the

1

organism, in this case, the Human Immuno-deficiency Virus (HIV). More plainly I have tested positive for HIV and subsequently cannot be allowed entry into the USA.

Marilyn, I need not exaggerate the kind of shock I received from this revelation, suffice to mention that it is a fatal blow to my person; as lethal as the disease that is to follow. Why? – I had never come to imagine, remotely or otherwise, that AIDS as a disease could afflict people like myself. At the back of my mind, AIDS has always been somewhat for 'those' people, far removed from healthy, intelligent and beautiful persons like myself. I can't help thinking that there must be a gross mistake somewhere for the simple reason that I believe, I – Catherine Njeri – can never be an AIDS victim.

Yet, between Friday and this Monday that I am writing, I have learnt better than that. I know that the AIDS virus is as indiscriminating as death itself. It closes its eyes to beauty, intelligence, wealth, status and what-have-you. Like a blind beggar, it can stop by anybody. It exploits human weaknesses and thrives at levels in which human sexual and social behaviour are a mockery to morality. Soon, human beings will be reduced to slaves of this virus. It laughs at the number of medical laboratories showing keen interest in it the entire world over. It equally laughs at the number of lives it claims each year that are a testimony to the havoc it is capable of wreaking within one single decade.

Now, it looks me in the face with a devilish smile of work well done – one more recruited for the world of the dead. I want to scream and hide, or run away to some far away planet where the virus is still alien. Better still, I want to rewind the clock of my entire life so that I could start anew next time, careful enough not to make the mistakes I have made.

I cannot fathom the idea, but an AIDS victim! – that is what I am now. Pretty soon I will be faceless and nameless.

Catherine, the beautiful name my mother gave me, will only be mentioned in hushed voices and by wagging tongues.

'You know Catherine, don't you? She has AIDS.' And this will make a lively story; something to gossip about among my circle of relatives, friends and acquaintances. And the rumour will make its rounds at a speed which lightning will envy. I can even foresee strange faces casting an ugly look my way. This is the stage I fear most and I do not think I will be able to bear the scandals and scorn, for mine is a delicate heart. It could quite easily break into pieces, or give way to a heart attack.

I can't help wishing all this was happening to someone else unknown to me, some sort of two-headed human being unfit to live with the rest of humanity. Wild thoughts these are, aren't they? To say the truth, my thoughts are quite agonising. In order to get a bit of relief they wander wildly over all possibilities and impossibilities. The minute they remain fixed on my dilemma, I get such a depressing feeling.

How I wish I was as strong and courageous as America's basketball hero, Magic Johnson, or as Uganda's Phili Lutaya! Where on earth did they get the courage to make public declarations of such a misfortune? I prefer to remain as silent and discrete as possible about my condition now until the symptoms develop and make it impossible for the secrecy to be maintained. I think this way, I will prevent myself from being stigmatised in society while I am still in the healthy carrier stage. But one thing I will not do is to help spread the virus through sexual contact with men. The guilt I would feel would kill me faster than the disease itself. I would be as guilty of murder as any murderer on the loose.

Marilyn, you are a dear person to me that is why, with good reason, I choose to address this letter to you. You have proved to be such a valuable and selfless friend in high school, campus and thereafter. We have literally shared the memorable moments of our adult life together until nine months ago, when you left for the Netherlands in pursuit of further education. Even then, we still share our thoughts through lively communication in the form of long letters which could easily pass for pamphlets. And you are such a talented writer. You describe everything so finely and in such detail, from the horrible winters to the slow pace of social life in Holland. Your letters are such fun – they always make my day when they appear monthly.

Another reason why I address this unique letter to you is that I do not want the news of my condition to reach you through hearsay, so that you have to learn it from Rosemary, Viola, Janet or the whole lot of them. The shock will be greater that way, and the news will be impersonal. By writing straight to you, you will be able to understand more clearly the story of my life and the gruesome hours I have to pass with the knowledge that I am an AIDS victim. I am aware that the story of my life is not so extraordinary as to warrant attention; rather, it is its similarity with the day to day lives of other girls growing up that makes it worth narrating. It is a clear demonstration that AIDS is a reality, and that it is not far removed from our pattern of life. I have mentioned that mine is a human tragedy. Let me also add that it is in particular, the tragedy of youth and women in Africa who risk being exposed to the virus daily. Mine is not a selfish lament or cry for my shortened life and obliterated future. It is a cry for the masses who fall victims yearly, and a decry for those among us who stick to high risk behaviour. It is like a cry of a nation which has been defeated at war.

I write so that from my experience, you – and hopefully through you many others – may benefit and learn to avoid the mistakes I have made. And the first lesson is that AIDS is a reality, a terrible disease whose wages are death.

For three days now my mind has run through all the alternative ways in which I could lead the remaining months or years of my life as soberly and decently as possible. I am ashamed to mention that in the dark of the cold still nights I

4

have even contemplated the suicide possibility. But what would happen to baby Jimmy, considering that I am a single parent? I am also not daring enough to take my own life. As it is I am afraid of harbouring the AIDS virus because I am afraid of dying. Why then, should I give myself away to suicide which will kill me faster than AIDS? Fortunately, I am not the suicidal type. I value the right to life. And who knows, I console myself, maybe the wonder drug will be discovered soon before the AIDS disease can eat me away.

Up to this stage, I have not found enough courage to disclose to anybody that I have tested positive for the virus. I cannot even bring myself to inform Alex, who might be as hard hit with the news as I am. The misfortune is that he too could be a victim as he has been my sexual partner for about three years now. Writing to Brian, the father of my son, is ridiculous and out of the question. He sounded the AIDS alarm which I did not heed. He would only laugh at me.

I have already requested for a study leave at my place of work. How do I explain to my employers that I cannot travel after all and that I wish to retain my job? What do I tell my parents, who are already making a proud show in the village, happily telling everyone that their daughter is travelling overseas for further studies? Marilyn, how do I disentangle myself from this big mess and continue to live as if nothing has happened?

I sit here all day long and brood. I look around the house and suddenly it is not like my house any more. Everything looks different, as if silently mocking me. The wardrobe looks strange and I suddenly hate all those clothes in it. The radio does not play anymore – even music not meant to be sad now sounds melancholic. I walk up and down the house, torn with pain, and lie down and get up again dozens of times. I try to read or knit, but in vain. I feel regret, bewilderment and suffering. I am angry at myself, angry at Alex, even angry at the entire world. The sun does not seem to reach me; it is as if it has suddenly disappeared at high noon. It cannot possibly be the same sun that has shone over the twenty eight years of my life.

I have cried a lot too. Tears of rage, of grief, of pity – and of shame. The tears flow easily now, with nobody to wipe them. I cannot recall the last time I had a meal. At this time of writing, five cups of unfinished coffee glare at me on the kitchen table. Hunger is almost alien to me; as alien as the depressing news is.

I am now afraid of everything – of a cat, of walking out of the house, receiving visitors, answering the phone. It could be Alex on the other end chatting away happily; 'Hi Honey . . . could we meet on Wednesday at the usual place, say six o'clock?' or it could be Frank, George, Jimmy or anybody at that.

I have not recovered from the shock enough to assume that nothing has changed. Brian liked quoting that wise saying that *'facts do not cease to exist just because they are ignored'*. I have been able to ignore other facts easily, but can one ignore the fact that one is at the end of life? I do not think I could. I know I will find it extremely difficult to go about life in the face of the new development. I therefore need plenty of time to reflect and get used to my new self, just as a prisoner who with time, becomes fond of a spider.

*   *   *

Two weeks have now elapsed since I started writing this letter. Somehow the dark clouds which seemed to hide the sun from me have partly drifted and I am now feeling much lighter at heart. Within this time, I have tried to lay my hands on any information I could get on AIDS. I am surprised at how little I knew previously about the virus and the disease. I have even been bold enough to face my doctor with the news that I had tested positive for the AIDS virus. At worst, he has confirmed the results, which cuts the last thread of hope that I was hanging on to.

6

The ELISA test employed, the doctor says, does not detect the presence of the AIDS virus in the blood. It only detects if antibodies have been produced in response to the virus. If the test is positive, it shows that the victim has been exposed to the virus. It is therefore assumed that the virus is present in the victim, as is the case with me now. From the pamphlet I have, ELISA is an abbreviation for Enzyme-Linked Immunosorbent Assay, whatever that means.

'Is there a way of knowing how long I have been harbouring the virus?' I asked in a shaking voice.

'Not any that I know of.' The doctor answered, removing the stethoscope from his neck and placing it on the table. Then, as an afterthought he added, 'The only tangible information we can go by is that it must be over three months ago'.

'Why three months?' I wanted to know.

'Because sero-conversion commonly occurs six to twelve weeks after infection. This is when the antibodies appear in the victims serum. If a person is found to have antibodies in his blood, we say that he has sero-converted or that he is seropositive. You have obviously sero-converted that is why I say you could have contracted the virus probably more than twelve weeks ago.'

'How can a person know that he has undergone sero-conversion without necessarily coming for the test?'

'Well, it is difficult to guess that one is undergoing sero-conversion. In some cases, it has been noted that sero-conversion may be accompanied by clinical signs and symptoms such as fever, swelling of lymph glands, night sweats, headache and cough. But then you appreciate that most of these symptoms are so common, that a victim would not associate them with any serious condition. Some victims have been found not to possess any of the symptoms previously. A good number will remain symptom-free through the sero-conversion phase.'

'What stage am I undergoing now?' I asked, shifting uneasily in my chair as though I were sitting on a crown of thorns.

'Are you experiencing fevers, night sweats, diarrhoea or any ailment at all?'

I shook my head without offering a reply.

'Good', he said, as though acquitting me of AIDS. 'Then you could still be in the healthy carrier stage. Some people choose to call it the latent phase or the asymptomatic phase. In this period, there are no symptoms and the person is quite well but infectious.'

'How long can one last in this latent phase?'

'Up to seven or eight years if you are lucky. The period varies from one individual to another. In some unfortunate cases it could be as little as six months.'

'What happens after this? I mean which phase follows?' I was curious to know.

'After the asymptomatic phase the victim may progress over a variable time to pre-AIDS conditions or to fully expressed AIDS. In both cases the victim suffers from symptoms which vary in severity.'

I wanted to ask what he meant by pre-AIDS conditions, but decided to ask more worrying questions.

'How long then can a patient last after he has developed symptoms of the AIDS disease?'

'A matter of months, say eight or so, depending on a number of factors. Very few patients with fully expressed AIDS have been known to last longer than two years.'

'Is there any hope for discovery of the AIDS cure in my time?' I asked, sounding desperate.

'That my dear lady, is what we all hope for. It keeps medical researchers busy in their laboratories long after the last resident has put his lights off. What we still do not know is when they will make a break-through. For now, we have to face the harsh reality that there is no known cure for AIDS. The only salvation for mankind is for its people to avoid high risk behaviour and live as morally upright as monks and nuns.' He said the last sentence sounding like a preacher who ends the sermon as he closes his Bible.

I thanked him for his time and left the clinic with my head buzzing. How strange this world is – Catherine discussing AIDS instead of fixing an appointment for a date out! Thank God there is writing to do. It helps me fill in the long hours I would otherwise spend crying and worrying. Right now I am a strange mixture of hurt pride and frustrated ambitions that are still sufficiently alive. I live by the hour, hoping that there might possibly be a silver lining to the cloud, someday.

Chapter Two

Twenty eight years ago, on a cold September night, I am told, a baby girl had her first kicks of life in the small village of Kamacharia in Murang'a district. The little girl, the only one among four boys, was christened Catherine Njeri.

Mother treated me with excessive affection. This, I guess, so much infuriated my brothers that by the time I was five years old, I was the target of their pinchings and beatings. They never seemed to miss an opportunity to pull my hair and knock my head whenever Mother was out of sight. And soon I learnt to revenge by fighting back.

Father owned a bookshop in Murang'a town and was largely absent from home. He does not stir any memories in my early childhood. When I started being aware of him, he was always the cold unfriendly stranger who sat quietly in an armchair with one eye on the newspaper and the other on trouble makers. Mother never appeared to be happy whenever he was around and us children went to lengths to keep out of his sight. With time, I started regarding him in silent loathing. I vaguely remember a fight my parents had when I was seven which made us cry and huddle in the corner of the bedroom. I still recall how my mother sobbed all night after my father had proudly walked out of the house with the door banged shut behind him.

Against this background, there developed in me a strong resentment towards men that by the time I was admitted to a local primary school, I was involved in many fights with the boy pupils. That is how I landed myself in a girls only boarding school at the tender age of ten.

Unlike most other boarders, I adored boarding school, probably for its absence of fighting boys. The school was run by missionary sisters and the code of conduct was strict. Once, I was caught fighting with one of the girls in the senior classes over a playing marble and we were both heavily punished. Besides washing the school cathedral, we were threatened with suspension. I hated the idea of going home and so I apologised to the sister in charge of discipline and promised to be good. I guess the incident marked the beginning of my being sociable. During the years that followed, I made lots of friends and improved my grades in class tremendously. By the time I reached standard six, I was a darling to the teachers and many pupils.

At about the same time, something terrible happened. My father's relationship with Mother took a nose dive when he married a second wife. In one of their frequent quarrels he had threatened to discontinue paying our school fees and extending any financial help to Mother. I cried myself to sleep that night after I had received the news in a letter from Mother. But she forgot to mention one thing, that the step-mother had come home with her two sons. I got this additional information on a later day in a letter from one of my brothers.

Fortunately, I channeled my frustrations into increased classroom concentration and serious study. The results could not have been much better. That term, I attained the coveted first position in my class, leading thirty four other students. Only then I was not happy that the term had come to an end. The thought of going home in the mess that prevailed there was disheartening. I saw how other pupils sang for days on end about their sweet home while poor me brooded over the prospect of meeting and coping with a step-mother and an extra pair of boys. At that time, my sorrow knew no bounds.

Well, as good fortune had it, my step-mother and her sons were not at home the Saturday evening I arrived from school. I learnt that they had gone to harvest tea on their farm at Kanyenya-ini, and would probably be back the following day. I was greatly relieved as it gave me time enough to recollect myself. My brothers quickly fed me on the details of the latest developments. Ever since I had gone to boarding school they were more friendly, especially for the first few days of the holiday. They said the other boys, Maina and Wachira, were very friendly. The problem, they said, was Father who they had nicknamed 'the roaring lion of Judah' for their own good reasons.

The home breaker did not show up until the following Tuesday and when she did, all my reservations about her were swept away with the wind. For accompanying her was one of the most handsome boys I had ever seen. Maina, for that was his name, appeared to be my agemate or slightly older. Wachira, the younger of the two, was not nearly as handsome as the brother but with time, he proved to be more talkative and friendly. In the course of that week, I had established a rapport with the two, to the extent I had not been able to with my brothers. I talked about boarding school for hours on end, and they always wanted to hear some more.

While all this was happening my mother was not amused and cautioned me to have very few dealings with the other family. I always countered, saying that we were studying together. Maina was in standard seven then and sounded quite brilliant to me.

Marilyn, if there is anything known as a crush, then granted, I had a bad one on Maina. It was at this time that I started being aware of myself. I took a lot of caution in dressing and fixing my hair, spending hours on end at the mirror. I cite this incident because it reflects a clear departure from my childhood repulsion of boys to the teenage realization that I was a beautiful girl capable of being loved by those very boys.

Most of the time I was left at home to undertake household duties while my mother and brothers went to the farm, so I had plenty of time with Maina and Wachira. My step-mother also developed a liking for me and I could have melted the day she told me that I was a very pretty girl. I cannot recall the circumstances, but I couldn't help wishing that phrase had come from Maina.

The April holiday quickly passed by without much event and soon, it was time again to go back to school. Father had not enforced the sanctions on payment of school fees, so Mother had told me, but by this time I could have given anything to be left to attend the local primary school together with my step-brothers.

On my last Sunday at home, I stayed behind to do my packing as my mother and brothers went to church. While busy packing, I suddenly noticed Maina open my bedroom door. This was the first time Maina had come to my bedroom despite much persuasion previously.

Now as he stood there at the doorway, we just stared at each other for minutes on end amid the wild palpitations of my heart. Before I could find voice, he remarked with a slight note of disgust; 'So you have decided to go back to boarding school?' We had discussed the possibility of my staying back to attend the local school to reduce the school fees burden on my mother.

'You know Maina I have no choice. Father is willing to pay my fees and Mother is impressed by my performance in school.'

'But I heard that attending boarding school was initially your idea.'

'That was three years ago. Then, home was different.'

We considered each other silently for a long time before I could resume my packing. Meanwhile Maina walked from the door, closing it behind him and sat on my bed as if it was the most natural thing to do. I swear it could have been, to me, a scene from Hollywood.

'You know Catherine, this place will not be the same without you'. He paused for effect and when I volunteered no reply, he went on, 'Already, Wachira is complaining.'

'Wachira complaining? Why should he be complaining?'

'I think he likes you very much. In fact he is in love with you but doesn't know how to approach you on the issue.'

'You can't be serious.' I said dropping the skirt I had started to fold.

'You love him too, don't you?' Maina again, this time he was watching me closely.

At this stage I wanted to hide from him. Surely he hadn't noticed that it was he, Maina, I loved and not the brother? As I stood there transfixed, unable to answer him, he threw in the bait.

'You know you are beautiful Catherine. I wouldn't blame him anyway.' He said this standing up as if preparing to go.

Within no time, without knowing who did what, we were in each other's arms, kissing. For a couple of minutes we just stood there kissing and embracing. I had never been kissed by anyone before and though I had listened to my schoolmates chattering about a shameless girl who allowed herself to be kissed on the mouth by boys, I had no idea what a kiss was like. Indeed for several months following this first kiss, I was under the delusion that it was Maina's own marvelous invention.

I did not want the rest of my family to come from church and find Maina in my room so I quickly disentangled myself and requested him to leave. After straightening his shirt and neatly brushing his hair Maina held my hand, kissed it and muttered something to the effect that he would miss me terribly. I echoed the same and promised to write once I got to school. So that is the way it all began between boys and me.

I won't go into the details of how long it took me to pack, the number of glasses I broke that evening and how many sleepless nights followed this first encounter with Maina. You too must have gone through similar experiences but

14

note that in the whole of my life with men I have never loved anybody as intensely as I did Maina. You know all that rapport with a first love – or is it first infatuation?

Of course after I had gone to school we did exchange all those sweet-for-nothing letters pledging undying love. This is the period of time I like to remember most. It was to mark, years later, the ideal romance to which all others would be compared in my constant quest for true love.

I have never stopped to wonder why Maina never suggested, or acted in a manner to suggest, sexual involvement as we kissed this first time and several other times during the holidays that followed. Was it that we were far too young to be involved sexually, or did the brotherhood factor come into play?

I am not trying to suggest that I was ready to go all the way by any means; rather, after my long experience with boys (call them men if they want), I have not come across one other who will not have sex at the top of his mind once we are left alone in the privacy of the bedroom. Among all the boys I have had even the slightest involvement with, none – with the exception of Maina – has been content enough to stop at kissing or holding hands.

After my relationship with Maina had been terminated, and following the onset of dating other boys, this thing worried me quite a lot. It was only much later, after I had read about the anatomical differences between men and women with regard to sexual arousal and response, that I began to understand why boys just won't stop at kissing.

It was with Maina I first discovered the pleasure and satisfaction of loving and being loved, and that lingering kiss remains one of the most beautiful things that happened to me in my early life.

15

Chapter Three

My relationship with Maina lasted for little more than a year
and when it did end, both of us were left heartbroken. At
that time, I had only four months to my Certificate of Primary
Education national examination. Maina had performed
excellently in the same examination and received admission
to Mang'u High School, Thika, one of the leading boys'
schools in Kenya.

We had been in constant communication from the onset of
our 'friendship' so each of us had accumulated a sack of
letters from the other. It was to be these same sweetly
worded letters that would lead us to a forced separation
after their discovery by my mother. Maina always wrote
romantic letters. A typical letter always started with 'Honey'
and ended with 'Honey is sweet, my love, but not as sweet
as you are'. I had been foolish enough to come home with
all these letters and carefully tuck them in my school bag
without much thought of their possible discovery.

I hate to recall that black Saturday evening we were
summoned to appear before our parents to answer charges
as though we were suspects before a court of law.

We both declined to answer any questions on the nature of
our relationship and insisted that the discovered letters were
from another Maina. What a frail excuse that was, but what
more could you expect of thirteen year olds?

Maina was made to bring at least three of his exercise
books for comparison of handwriting. It turned out to be as
similar as siamese twins.

Without dwelling on the petty details, my 'affair' with Maina
ended that evening after we each received a baptism of six
strokes of the cane, uncountable slaps and made a promise
never to repeat the same again. It was the 'roaring lion of
Judah' at his best. Father said he would see to it that we
never spent another holiday together. Besides, he was to

give my headmistress authority to unseal and read all the letters addressed to me before passing them down to me.

Mother in turn, broke into a stern lecture on pre-marital sex and pregnancy in girls. She mentioned some of the girls in the village whose schooling had been discontinued on grounds of pregnancy. Had anything in those letters pointed towards sex, I wondered? The truth is, just as I have admitted before, we had never engaged in sex or even discussed the possibility of sexual involvement. According to Mother, befriending a boy was tantamount to getting pregnant. How misinformed!

Marilyn, at this stage I will briefly mention something about lack of appropriate sex education in many Kenyan families. Most of the girls I went to school with complained of deteriorating relationships between their parents and themselves especially during the adolescent stage. More than one girl pointed out that all their parents did was to threaten that involvement with boys would lead to misery. They never as much as discussed the changes the girls were undergoing and how to cope with the outburst of emotions in adolescence.

Mothers were rated poor sex educators. A number of girls admitted shyly that they never received any prior information on menstruation from their mothers – they just happened upon it, thanks to the boarding schools. One girl narrated to us how her mother had bought for her a packet of tampons along with her other shopping for the term. She had counter checked against the list she had written for the shopping and satisfied that it was an additional item, she decided to ask her mother about it. 'You are a girl. You will soon discover what it is,' was all her mother could tell her.

I also remember, while in high school, the sad story of a girl who was locked in the house, along with her sisters, throughout the holidays for fear that they would get to know boys and get pregnant. They were not allowed to socialise and their brothers could only meet their peers outside the compound gates. Her father carried the keys to the huge padlock with him. The girl's attitude towards her father was outrageous and she kept threatening to teach him a lesson or two. Immediately after her fourth form examinations she eloped with the first man in sight. One of her sisters, she had said, had her uterus removed at the age of seventeen for fear of facing her parents with a pregnancy.

You must know of many other incidences where girls suffer in the process of growing up. In general, they point to an obvious lack of basic sex education from the parents. I can confidently attribute to this the increase in abortions and pregnancies among adolescents. Now with the AIDS dimension added, the picture is pretty grim. I will come back to this point in my narrations of adolescence.

For a few days following that black Saturday and prior to our travelling back to our respective schools, I spent most of the time in my room brooding. The idea of losing Maina's friendship was simply untenable and the heart in my chest grew sick with pain and felt heavy as if bound with lead. When I did go back to school, I wrote Maina two letters lamenting our ended affair and the stupid way our parents had handled us. I promised that I would never forget the sweet memorable days of our relationship, especially the few occasions we had kissed and embraced. Now fifteen years later, I am sure, Maina would be happy to learn that I kept this promise. Of course Maina was not supposed to reply to my letters so I have never known, to this day, how he felt about our separation. At the time I am writing Maina is happily married with one child.

When the time came for me to sit for the exams, I was prepared enough and did so with a strong determination to perform even better than Maina. Unlike all other disappointments that year, the results were a glowing success.

I had deliberately chosen schools far away from home and thus received with joy the news that I had been admitted to the then Highlands Girls' School, Eldoret (now Moi Girls' High School). The first two years in secondary school were uneventful. Then, towards the end of second form my heart jolted again. This time I had developed another 'crush' over a new teacher who had been sent to our school and was taking my class for maths and chemistry. Not only was he handsome and gentlemanly, but he was quite thorough in his teaching. Before long, he was the talk of our class and even those girls who had given up on those two subjects started showing interest.

I was on the more quiet and reserved side so I listened with burning envy to the more aggressive girls quip; 'Today he couldn't keep his eyes off me', and again, 'Didn't you see the way he looked at me as I stood up to clean the board?'

Unlike Maina's case in which I was the sole competitor, I knew I would have no hope this time and regarded the other girls who had openly shown interest with a lot of jealousy. I could certainly not compete with them on grounds of aggressiveness and so decided that my only weapon would be to perform well in this teacher's subjects. But as I laid my strategies, my competitors grew more aggressive in their means. One afternoon during that teacher's lesson, I was surprised to see one of the girls had completely unbuttoned her blouse, thus exposing a good part of her naked chest. I kept looking from Sarah to the teacher who seemed quite engrossed in his teaching. He was hardly the type to get angry with us but I kept hoping that this time, his anger would snap. To my dismay, the lesson ended without any hitch and I could have hit the roof when the teacher picked up his books from the teacher's desk, smiled in Sarah's direction and walked out. You should have seen Sarah's beaming face as she buttoned up, ready to sleep throughout a lady teacher's CRE lesson.

My heart sank further when about two weeks later, I noticed Sarah sneak out of the teacher's house one early morning.

Marilyn, since this incident, men have never stopped intriguing me. Just when you expect a perfect gentleman to go after decent girls, he does quite the reverse. Does this also explain why some seemingly good husbands abandon their decent and faithful wives and go for scantily dressed, crazy-looking girls picked by the roadside, in the bars or some other ungodly places? No wonder there is a speedy circulation of AIDS and other STD's.

The third form saw me join a number of school clubs for the main reason of getting a chance to participate in innings and outings involving boys' schools. As it was, the adolescent stage was taking its toll among my agemates, and I was no exception. I envied those who had boyfriends and publicly mentioned Maina as my boyfriend so that I was not left out on the list. Deep down, I knew my relationship with Maina was over. I yearned for somebody to fill the gap Maina had left and joining the clubs seemed to offer such a possibility. I joined choir, mathematics and debating clubs. Mother had urged me to join the Christian Union but at that time I felt it would get in my way and shatter my hopes of acquiring a boyfriend. By this time, I had come to the conclusion that being a good straight girl did not quite pay. A little aggressiveness here and there was desirable. After all hadn't it won Sarah a handsome teacher?

My first outing was to the Rift Valley Technical School where we went as a mathematics club. I had taken great pains to dress neatly and make a hairstyle that even Madonna could have envied. The day turned out to be a disappointment. I had talked to a number of boys over refreshments and lunch, but none of them aroused my interest. In fact, it appeared as though only the uglier boys were approaching me while the handsome ones talked to the girls who had taken an active role in the discussions. I returned to school a very disappointed girl.

During the final term of the year, our debating club received an invitation to Saint Patrick's, Iten. This aroused my wild expectations – I had always wanted to go to Iten as a joy rider previously but I was never lucky. I had been very active in the debating club and it came as no wonder when my name was proposed to be among the main speakers. The idea was chilling at first but soon I became resigned to it, seeing it as a chance to win a boyfriend.

I was so restless the week before the outing as I tried to improve on my oratory skills. More worrying was the embarrassment of my worn out school shoes so I set out to borrow from my friend who had an extra neat pair. I also needed a nice hair clip to hold back my hair, as I had seen other girls do, so that it could look neat and simple. No crazy hairstyle this time. I was fortunate to get these two things through borrowing, thanks again to boarding school.

Come Saturday and I was all set. I offered many silent prayers to God so that this time I would not return empty handed. In the bus, on our way to Iten, I went over the points I had memorised. I was everything but nervous. We arrived slightly before eleven and were shown around the school compound. There was this guy taking me around who, for lack of something to say, introduced even the maize plants in their school garden; 'And this is maize, we plant it in our school garden'. I couldn't control my laughter.

After this familiarization tour we were taken to the hall where the debate was to take place and I was pleased to note that chairs had been reserved for the main speakers at the front of the hall. Once we were seated, there was a welcoming speech by the patron after which the motion was moved by the chairpersons of the two respective clubs.

When my turn came to propose the motion, I confidently stood up and presented my arguments with the eloquence of a street preacher. I cannot recall the phrasing of the argument but I can vividly remember the wild applause I received at the end of my presentation. I was elated.

At the time for refreshments a cool 'saint' came to sit next to me. He was quite handsome, I admit. He told me he had liked my arguments which he considered brilliant. We talked a bit more about the lively debate and then the conversation drifted to ourselves.

It did not take long to find out that Henry was on the list of the most coveted boys at the school. After the refreshments, one of the senior girls had told me, in whispers, that I had managed to catch one of the big fishes from the pond. I did not understand why Henry was referred to as a big fish then, but the truth did not take long to surface. That afternoon, before going back to our school, we had a dance during which I paired up with Henry again.

'Where have you been all my life?' he murmured as we danced to a certain record.

'You know Cathy I could have easily mistaken you for an angel had it not been for your uniform,' he had said again. I was, like many other innocent adolescents, hearing these words for the first time and, juxtaposed with the soft music and Henry's hands over my waist, there couldn't have been a better name to give to love.

Henry had dark handsome features, was tall, and standing six inches above my five feet height, he easily filled in for the man of my dreams. He looked exceptionally charming on that day in his green cardigan and grey trousers and to date, I can still give an accurate description of how Henry looked.

As we danced to the last record, the electricity between us intensified as Henry held me closer whispering that he had fallen in love with me at first sight and pleaded that I accept him as a boyfriend – would I mind?

22

Henry's approach swept me completely off my feet. For all I cared, I could have been some astronaut in a rocket to Mars, Jupiter or some undiscovered planet, but not an innocent schoolgirl standing there feeling so loved.

I did not, however, want to sound outrightly cheap and so I promised to make up my mind and send him the verdict. He urged me not to keep him waiting for long.

On our way back, the girl seated next to me in the school bus asked; 'So you succeeded in hooking the tycoon's son?'

'Is Henry a tycoon's son?' I returned the question.

She looked me over for a fraction of a second as though trying to read my mind and, satisfied that I was innocent in my questioning, she talked on.

'Don't you know Henry's dad owns half of Eldoret town?'

'If at all he does,' I replied, 'Henry mentioned nothing about it. Only said he comes from around Eldoret town.'

'But I have always known Henry to be a braggart. How could he have not told you all that?'

'He did not sound like a brag to me.' I paused and when she did not comment, I added, 'How well do you know Henry?' From her expressionless face, I could guess that she probably had never talked to Henry in person.

'I know him so well,' she said after a while. 'He is always bragging about his dad, their car, their large farmhouse and a lot of other bullshit.'

I chose not to comment because I did not like the conversation. I knew that however badly anybody talked of Henry at that time, I was not going to take it in for I was tuned to a different wavelength. The words of the last record we had danced to were still fresh in my mind and it seemed to me I had at last found a new Maina.

That night, I scribbled in my diary, 'Welcome into my life, Henry. Maina can now rest in peace.'

23

I still have that diary up to this day and I have never stopped laughing at my stupidity whenever I read this entry. It reflects the vulnerability of a curious adolescent girl initiating a relationship that may mean the whole world then, only to prove insignificant years later.

And you can bet on how difficult it is to dissuade a girl who has fallen in love in this manner from such a relationship whether by coercion or through counselling.

I was sixteen at the time I met Henry, that honey-tongued son of an illiterate tycoon. The adolescent flame in me was ablaze when, hardly a week after the outing, I wrote to Henry declaring I was all his. I can imagine the wide grin he could have given upon reading these words. Within no time we had exchanged photographs, letters 'with lots of hugs and kisses'. This was a favourite way to conclude the letters. I guess it was the in-thing those days. In his first letter, Henry had indicated his hobbies as basketball, dancing, surfing and skating. Looking back, I can see that he would have been more convincing were he writing from some temperate continent, probably Europe or America. Skating in equatorial Africa? As for basketball, I soon found out that he had never been seen on the basketball pitch. I guess he did not even know the difference between a basketball and a football.

Then, Henry was seventeen and doing his fourth form. He did not try to hide from me the fact that it could not matter less whether or not he passed his examination. Rather, as the examination period drew closer, he had a brighter idea. Could I possibly delay my going home for the Christmas holiday by one day, so that we could have some time for ourselves? He promised he would not detain me a day more.

This notice came early enough and so after weighing all factors, love weighed the heaviest and I decided this was the only chance I had to have fun.

As soon as our closing date was made known to us, I wrote confidently to Mother moving the date forward by a day. I thought myself very clever after this smart move. I then wrote to Henry confirming that I would be staying over and started the countdown to the closing date. I am sure in my fantasy, the idea of sex never featured. Maina had taught me that one could have a relationship with a boy without any sexual involvement, and I did not have the slightest inkling that the rest would be markedly different.

I did the end of year exams in a state of euphoria as the countdown narrowed down to one week, then a few days and finally whamo! 'Henry here we go!'

Never in the history of my schooling had I performed so dismally in my exams as I did that term. My class teacher wrote a terse remark; 'Wake up Catherine!' Thank God my parents were not overly keen on having the report forms; they never got to have a look at this one.

We had ruled out Henry coming to pick me up from school so instead I walked to town with my bags and headed straight for the Mid-nite Cafe where we had arranged to meet. As I approached the cafe, I noticed Henry seated in a cool blue Peugeot 504 saloon. On seeing me, he came out of the car with the charm and gaiety comparable to that of Eddy Murphy in *Coming to America*. We exchanged greetings after which he took my bags and kept them in the car boot.

'We could have some snacks in here,' he said, leading the way into the cafe. Over snacks we talked about the abhorred exams and then, school life in general. Henry had finished his exams two days earlier and he chatted happily about how he had burnt his school books and dumped his school uniform in an old box at home. He said he hated school and was positive he did not want to go on with it.

The conversation switched on to 'old guy, our car, our farm, our bla-bla-bla.' So Henry was a brag after all.

What was I supposed to talk about? Our quarter-acre farm and its meagre produce? Our roof-leaking semi-permanent house that was not worth a second glance? The trouble my mother went through to have us eat one decent meal? I would be damned if I had anything at all I could brag about to Henry, so I listened with feigned attentiveness as he talked about their wealth.

After clearing our snacks, Henry paid the bill and we got into 'our car'. He informed me that we would go to a restaurant in Eldoret for our lunch.

As he started the engine, he asked casually, 'Cathy, do you drink?'

'Drink what?' I asked with pretended innocence.

'Alcohol of course. Any alcohol – be it wine, whisky, beer and the likes.

I answered truthfully that I had never taken alcohol. I did not tell him I did not even know the difference between wine and whisky. I was not even sure if I had seen any.

'That's strange,' he said. 'All the girls I know take some Kingfisher or Woodpecker over lunches.' He went on.

Some kinds of birds? I wondered silently as I pondered some more over the statement. He had a number of girlfriends then? No, it wasn't possible, another voice within me consoled. Hadn't he said, in one of his letters, that I was his one and only?

'I cannot possibly show you the whole of Eldoret town in one day, but I'll try to point out some good joints as we drive along,' he said interrupting my thoughts.

'Now, on our right across this road is Woodhouse. I occasionally come here for discos but I prefer the Opera to it. They have better music and most good looking chicks flock there.' That again, I said to myself. Outwardly, my face remained expressionless. He negotiated a corner and turned right.

26

'This one here is the Jambo Hotel, a good spot for chips. Across there is the Opera discotheque,' he drooled on, pointing at it.

I had heard many Eldoret-raised highlanders talk about the Opera. Their stories were exciting and full of saga. Now on this dull day, the Opera, with its dirty white painting and black-and-red writing looked miserable and lifeless. I could not believe all those fabulous tales had their origin in this building.

'Across the bus park, you can see the Miyako Hotel, my old man's drinking joint. He spends more time there than he ever spends at home.' Henry broke out into laughter.

'You should see him holding the paper upside down, pretending to be busy reading. Poor dad!'

That is how I came to conclude that the tycoon could be illiterate.

It seemed to be an eternity before we got to Eldoret West. Henry had entered into another monologue about his father's drinking habits and his young girlfriends who were treated to anything money could buy. As he parked the car, Henry explained that he had chosen that particular hotel because being out of town, the chances of bumping into his father or any member of the family were slim.

The hotel was fairly packed with middle-aged men and much younger ladies all drinking some kind of alcohol. A number of men were talking at the peak of their voices. Some winked at me as I faithfully walked behind Henry. How could he have chosen such a place? This was a pub, and not a restaurant as he had called it. Over the loud speakers Tabuley's music entertained the customers.

We settled at a table in the corner and I tried very hard to conceal my disappointment. A grey-aproned waitress came instantly to take our order. Henry requested me to take some wine but I insisted on plain cola. After the waitress had left, Henry persuaded me some more saying it was decent

27

to take some wine while the men took beer, and that he was there to take care of me if I did lose control.

'Look, all the ladies here are drinking something. You will be the only odd one out.'

He said he could afford anything for my sake, if it was the price I was afraid of. He was even wise enough to let me have a glimpse of his wallet. I remember wondering how a young boy like him could have so much money, no matter how rich his father was rumoured to be. Personally, I survived on pocket money of fifty shillings for a whole term and Mother never forgot to ask if I had some money left over upon closing.

In the end, Henry had his way, and my soda was mixed with increasing amounts of wine – or was it whisky? – as I gulped down one glass after another.

Our lunch of chips and chicken was served in between the drinking and pretty soon I was talking as much as Henry. He encouraged me to drink saying that I looked more beautiful in a light mood. I felt pure ecstasy.

Later on, we left the hotel and headed straight for a lodging in the town centre. After several kisses Henry left saying he was rushing the car home. He informed me that he wouldn't be long and urged me to take some more drinks, which we had carried along, to relax my mind while he was gone.

I must have fallen asleep instantly as I cannot recall having done a thing until Henry knocked at the door at six that evening.

Thus it was in this half-drunken state that I lost my virginity. If my classmates thought sex was their idea of fun, it certainly wasn't mine. To me, it was painful, and embarrassing, and wholly unsatisfying. I woke up the next day to the feeling of guilt and developed an impassioned hatred for Henry. He had told me to trust him as he would

28

not go all the way and he had mercilessly breached the trust.

I dressed hazily and took the first bus home, via Nairobi. By the time I arrived home, I had succeeded in pulling myself together outwardly. Yet, as I sat down at the table that evening, I had trembled lest my mother, unexpectedly endowed with powers of divination, might read on my face what had transpired. But very quickly, I realized that no one saw anything.

Then, of course, there was the worst of fears. I could be pregnant at the end of it all. At that time, there was nothing worse than pregnancy. I now remembered each word my mother had said about boys and pregnancy on that black Saturday when she had discovered love letters from Maina.

How I wished it was Maina who had done all that to me! But by that time, Maina was staying in Murang'a town. Father had not hesitated to rent a house in town for his second wife after our friendship with Maina had hit the dead end. I had not seen Maina ever since.

On my fourth day home I wrote a letter to Henry expressing fears that I could be pregnant and seeking his opinion and the reassurance of his love. Of course this time I had already decided that Henry and his money could go to hell, but I had not considered in the event of a pregnancy.

Hardly two weeks later, I received Henry's reply and could have fainted from shock as I was quite unprepared for the contents. I rewrite it here for your consideration.

Dear Catherine,

I was glad to learn that you reached home safely and had no problems with your parents. My dad sure raised hell when I finally got home that morning with my hair uncombed and shirt crumpled. I cooked up some explanation and he let me go.

I thought you would go home and forget about me so I got myself a new girlfriend called Nancy. Unlike

29

you, she is principled, won't take alcohol and enters
no hotel room. That's the kind of hot stuff I just need
to keep me going. I hope you will also get a man who
is good enough for you.

Bye for now.

Yours H.K.

I read that letter over and over again with the lump in my throat growing bigger and bigger until I broke into sobs. Nothing had been mentioned about the pregnancy. Thank God by some miracle I had gone through my period the previous week. I was now the unprincipled girl who agreed to take alcohol and go to a hotel room – changed overnight from the walking angel I had been to Henry. Jesus! He couldn't be serious.

I wanted to scream and vent anger on anything. I wrote several letters, full of abuse but fortunately tore them up each time. Somehow, I felt relieved after writing each letter.

And I started growing wise to the world of men after borrowing a single black sheet from Henry's book!

Chapter Four

I had never seen a real gun before. I opened my mouth to scream as the figure in black edged closer to the bed.

'No use screaming, Cathy,' Alex's voice came through, 'The quicker the means the better, ain't it?'

I sat up with a jolt as Alex stretched forward the hand with the gun. It was metallic grey in colour and I did not care about the other details.

'But why? Why should you want to kill me this way Alex?' I asked gasping.

'You bitch! How could you give me AIDS. You have ruined my life, that is why.'

He made as if to pull the trigger and this time I genuinely screamed . . .

I was soaked in beads of perspiration as I trembled to awareness. Where was Alex? I opened my eyes and realized that I had been dreaming. Thank goodness, I said. But then I remembered the events of the previous night and wanted to cling to sleep to avoid the reality.

Alex had taken me out, as is usually routine on Wednesday evenings, to the Rock Centre for goat roasting. This was the second time we were meeting after the shock of the AIDS news and I was debating within myself whether or not I could break the news to him. The doctor had said it would be wise to discuss the information with my sex partner and persuade him to go for a test himself. If by chance he was not yet infected, it could save his life.

I take alcoholic drinks on very few occasions such as on this day when I needed to gain the courage to break the sad news.

'What are you up to today, Catherine?' Alex could not help asking, 'You never take alcohol in the middle of the week!'

I informed him that I just wanted to feel good and that it wouldn't do any harm since I was still on my leave. Alex works in Nairobi but he comes fortnightly to Eldoret on business. Sometimes he comes in the middle of the week but mostly he comes on Fridays and stays over the weekend at my place.

I had found out from his identity card that he was thirty five years old although he looks much younger.

He had separated from his wife at about the time I had met him. I have never known what led to the separation because Alex talked very little about himself, but I gathered from speculation that it was over his extra-marital affairs. Besides me, I suspected he had another 'steady' in Nairobi. I was not sure whether they stayed together or lived separately.

We stayed out last evening until ten o'clock when Alex volunteered to drive me home. He said he was to join some friends at the White Castle pub.

'You don't mind coming in for a minute, do you?' I asked before he could stop the car engine.

'Then you have something to tell me?' He turned off the engine and walked out.

'I think there is something you ought to know that I have been holding back from you.' I said fumbling in my purse for my door keys. 'But it can wait if you are so much in a hurry.'

I managed to get the keys and thrust the appropriate one in the keyhole, all the time struggling to calm my nerves.

'What is it about?' Alex asked uneasily, almost impatiently. I had opened the door and now reached for the switch.

'That, you can find out in the warmth of the house, other than trembling out there in the cold.'

He looked at me for a few seconds and walked in. I was still standing by the switch with my handbag and so decided to close the door, all the time contemplating my next move. The heart in my chest was thumping loudly as I entered my bedroom to put away the handbag. How does one break such news, I wondered to myself. Yet, the earlier it was over with the better.

Meantime, Alex was pacing up and down the sitting room floor, scrutinising the pictures that hang neatly on the wall as if he were seeing them for the first time. He looked nervous as though he knew what to expect, or so I thought.

'Can we talk in the bedroom?' I requested.

This time he followed me without a word. He positioned himself at the edge of the bed. I sat in the middle facing Michael Jackson's poster which hung on the wall.

'What is it about?' Alex asked, sounding as if he hadn't just repeated the same question.

'I thought you would want to know.' I burst out without much ado, forgetting all the versions I had rehearsed. 'The results to my AIDS test showed positive and the doctor says it is good if you are informed as soon as possible. There is a possibility that you could be infected.'

The doctor, I remember had said it was easier to transmit the virus from man to woman than it was from woman to man.

Marilyn, it is difficult to describe the expression I saw on Alex's face, for all I know, it could have best been on the face of a dead man. I was sorry the minute those words were out of my mouth.

He remained silent and apparently composed for some ten minutes, all the while staring fixedly at the wardrobe. I looked up at Michael Jackson, half expecting the superstar to intervene. Instead, my eyes caught the words scribbled carelessly at one corner of the portrait; Who's Bad? Ironically, that seemed to be the question on our minds. When Alex did come round, he turned to me slowly with such rage that for a moment, I feared he would hit me.

Instead he said inarticulately, 'You bitch! You couldn't do any better than to ruin my life in this manner?'

I wasn't sure if it was a question or a statement. I said ten Hail Marys before finding my voice again.

'But you haven't been tested to know whether you are positive too. There just might be a chance that you have not been infected. But chances are, you could have passed on the infection to me.' This was like adding wood to the fire.

'You are not trying to say that I am the source of the virus, are you?' The tone of his voice was escalating. Alex had such quick tempers and I started fearing for my life.

'We can't rule that out,' my voice came out shakily. 'Only by testing negative can you be acquitted from blame,' I added, surprised at my guts.

'How did I ever get myself to be involved with this prostitute?' he said pointing a finger in my direction.

'Don't call me names, Alex. Can you explain to me how you are attracted to prostitutes. I guess your girlfriend in Nairobi is one hell of a prostitute too. A casanova – that's what you are.'

I am embarrassed to recollect the fight that followed. To be precise, it was an in-house *blitzkrieg*. I remember thinking that if Alex had been in possession of a gun, he would have shot me there and then. The cease-fire came shortly before midnight. There were two casualties. My cheeks were burning after the number of slaps I had received, my head ached too. Alex had attacked me as he would a male wrestler in the ring. Apart from biting his finger, he had gotten out of the mess with no injuries. The other casualty was the bed, which had partly served as a battlefield. It was totally wrecked. Last night I slept on the floor. I guess I will do the same tonight.

You should have heard me invoke the goddess of AIDS to wipe out the generations of men, such as Alex, who still inflict physical pain on women. I also told him to pray he died in a road accident on his way to Nairobi the next day. This way, I shouted, he would not have to face the reality of being an AIDS victim.

I was so angry Marilyn, I could have said anything. Little wonder it all came back in the nightmare.

Chapter Five

The moment I set my eyes on him I knew all my resolutions on men had gone down the drain. I know a handsome man when I see one, and the figure standing in front of me was a stereotype. He wore a white tee-shirt and a faded pair of jeans which reflected a man who took life lightly, or so I thought. His skin was the colour of a dairy milk chocolate, his brown eyes seemed to answer mine in an unmistakable acquiescence and when he did speak, his lips revealed a perfect set of white teeth.

'Frank didn't tell me he's staying with somebody,' he started off the conversation, I guess realising how dumbfounded I was.

'I haven't been here for long. I only arrived yesterday evening. Please come in.' I had almost forgotten the formalities.

'You don't mind letting a friendly fox into your hen house?' He asked humorously, at which we both laughed.

When he was seated I excused myself and dashed to the bedroom I was now using, suddenly aware of my dressing. I hesitated for a while, unsure of what to change into before settling for a purple dress which was simple enough.

As I took my seat in the sitting room, the stranger looked up from the newspaper he had been perusing and remarked casually.

'You now look fabulous, thanks to my coming here.' I could see he was the talking type and I also warmed to it.

'You aren't Frank's girlfriend, are you?'

'What if I am?' I tried pulling his leg.

'Then you might be in trouble with someone else I know.'

'With Sylvia?' I decided to surprise him. I knew Frank was going steady with a certain Sylvia, although we had never met.

'You know each other then?' the stranger could not hide his surprise.

I nodded, liking the conversation. It was relaxing for a start.

'What time are you expecting Frank?' he asked, looking at his own watch. From the clock on the wall, I could see it was approaching six. Frank could be here anytime now, I told the stranger.

'Frank is a very good friend of mine,' he talked on. 'He calls me Brain but my actual name is Brian. We were together in the University of Nairobi and have been fortunate to end up working in the same town.'

What was I expected to say. Introduce myself?

'My name is Cathy, short for Catherine. I am a young sister to Frank, which should answer your first question.' He seemed to brighten up or was I imagining it? We exchanged 'pleasures to meet you' and entered into a brief silence as butterflies churned in my stomach, growing bigger with each minute I sat facing Brian.

'You don't mind waiting for Frank do you?' I found my voice at last, 'In the meantime, I'll fix us some tea.'

'Good idea,' he said. 'And I'll play us some music, if you don't mind that is.' He was on the way to the cassette recorder.

'It's alright with me,' I answered feebly before making it to the kitchen.

'Cathy,' he called out immediately, arresting my movement on the corridor. I traced back my steps.

'I'll only serve as a DJ,' he said mischievously. 'Your choice please?'

'But you just said you will play us some music, go ahead with your own choice.'

'I am a gentleman, ladies first, they say.'

37

'Then in that case, play for me Donna Summer's *Unconditional love.*' He appeared contented as he fumbled through the cassettes and in another short while, the music came through.

I rushed into the kitchen not so much to make the tea as out of shyness. Music can have an electrifying effect and this is what I wanted to avoid. The scars I had sustained from Henry's relationship had not healed sufficiently. No man was going to open up the wounds. Then, there were my resolutions. My motto, after Henry, was simple and clear: *Keep away from men if you want to keep out of trouble.*

Yet, at that moment, I knew more than anything that my heart secretly yearned for a boyfriend to fill in the emptiness and the loneliness, so that I could be whole again. Granted the world of men was full of Henrys; but the Mainas? Were there also the Mainas? I wondered which camp Brian belonged to.

It took me almost an eternity to prepare the tea and assemble the cups. I had moments of abstraction when I could stand in front of the kitchen cupboard to get tea leaves or sugar and would completely forget what I was looking for.

'Cathy, are you around?' Brian's voice in the corridor surprised me. 'You choose a sentimental record and bury yourself in here leaving me to dance alone.' He accused, standing at the entrance of the kitchen.

'You couldn't have been dancing, were you?' I wanted to add that the song did not sound danceable to.

'Why not?' He said curtly. 'Need a helping hand?'

By then I was emptying the tea in the flask and with my mind in some kind of riot, failed to realize that the flask was full and that tea was trickling down it.

'Hey Cathy, watch out. The flask is full.' Brian alerted me.

'Stupid me.' What else could I have said to explain the mess?

'I will help take the tray of cups to the table.' Brian said wisely, as I started to clear the mess. Just supposing Frank was around? I thought to myself.

'You won't tell Frank?' my voice came out, begging.

'I understand,' he said with a note of affection. 'I nearly dropped the tray myself.' I guess he wanted to make me feel better. As we started to take the tea, he opened a new line of conversation.

'I am among the few African men who believe that a woman's place is not in the kitchen, but beside the man. I love to cook, hate doing dishes and can do almost anything in between.'

'You believe in the women's liberation movement then?'

That was our favourite topic of discussion, wasn't it Marilyn? Already, the world over, women were beginning to brace themselves for the International Conference on Women due to be held in Nairobi a year from then. I remember feeling proud of all those women who were lobbying for equality, among other women's rights. And we used to say someday we would be vocal leaders of the women's movement. A pity I may not live long enough to fulfil this ambition in Africa, where a majority of women still have their rights downtrodden and denied them. In some cases, the African man still regards the woman as some sort of sub-species which was created to serve him in all capacities in the house, entertain him in bed and procreate the number of children he would want. This same sub-species should be able to withstand the man's high affinity for other women, the man's thirsty throat for alcohol which can only be quenched at the expense of the household budget, and accept that her rightful place, over the centuries, remains the kitchen where she can only be seen and not heard. God forbid!

39

Now, listening to Brian show sympathy towards the woman's cause gave me such pleasure. Could he be married? He wore no ring but these days not many married people wear them afterall.

'Your wife must be very lucky then.' I said putting the litmus in the acid. The answer would be a sell-out, if he chose to answer that is. I hoped he would say what I wanted to hear most.

'There lies the problem.' He replied calmly. Even before he could complete his sentence I knew what he was to say next – he wasn't married after all. That gave me the hope that maybe someday, I would be wife to this handsome, empathetic man – I couldn't have asked for anything better!

Later on from his talk, I gathered that he worked as an entomologist for the Pyrethrum Board of Kenya, and that he was hopeful of winning a scholarship to further his studies abroad, preferably in Britain or America. I was tempted to ask him what he meant by 'entomologist' but refrained, not wanting to sound ignorant in front of him. In turn, I informed him that I had just completed my sixth form and was awaiting my exam results.

'I hope you don't mind my asking, but –' he hesitated for a while, replacing his unfinished cup of tea, as if unsure of what to say.

'Go ahead and ask.' I urged him on.

'What was it I wanted to ask? Ya, I wanted to know if you have a boyfriend.'

I was hoping that question would come, but now that it had, I did not know how to answer it. Giving a quick 'no' would imply keen interest. Hesitating would be taken to mean indecision, probably hatching a lie in my mind. I didn't have much time to run over the options and so I said, without batting an eyelid; 'You men are not worth having as boyfriends these days. You turn out to be such

40

disappointments and heartbreakers that in fact, women are better off left on their own.'

'Is that something you read somewhere and memorised or is it your formed opinion?'

'Take it whichever way it appeals to you.' I answered resignedly.

I had learnt a lot from Henry and was not about to give in easily to Brian despite the fact that I was at the end of my tether to have him. It had taken me a little over two years to get over the disappointment of Henry – a dull and listless period during which I tried in vain to understand men's actions. I was wise enough not to seek consolation in another pair of male arms over the remainder of my school period. This temporary abandonment of boys had given me plenty of time to concentrate on my academic work. And just as I had excelled in my CPE exams, I did meticulously well in the 'O' Level examinations attaining a First Division of fourteen points.

Subsequently, I was admitted to Nairobi Girls, which had been my second choice after Alliance Girls, where I did my 'A' Level. That is where I met you Marilyn. You sat one desk behind me remember? And you made it a habit to tap my back whenever a teacher had said something funny, or whenever you wanted to gossip. We exchanged letters received from boys, poured over past sagas and formed opinions together. You were always willing to share your bread with me over tea time and whenever I fell ill you took care of me. I had other friends too, but you remained steadfast throughout the two years I was at Nairobi Girls.

And here, I will rewrite what you scribbled in my autograph book towards the end of our term at the Nairobi Girls' School.

> "Cathy, watch out for the cunning man. Like a
> guerilla he lies still in the thick forest, waiting in

> *ambush. Do not fall for their honey talks or*
> *professed love. Fall for reason and for moral*
> *strength but never let emotion guide you.*
>
> *You are among the future women leaders.*
> *Hundreds of young women will want to follow*
> *your footsteps . . . only if you set an example to*
> *yourself by guarding your every moment."*

No advice, over the years has been more inspiring than this, Marilyn. I have not referred back to your text while writing. It is written all over my heart and it is to my regret that I never followed it after a while – maybe I wouldn't have ended up what I am today; an AIDS victim!

But as I talked to Brian that evening, I chose to guard my every moment, just as you had advised.

'Somebody must have hurt you so badly.' Brian was saying. 'A first love turned sour?'

He looked at me with his piercing eyes and I wanted to cry afresh, remembering Henry.

Aloud, I told him he would be better off making his choice of music than sitting there trying to get anything out of me. He obeyed and after placing a Don Williams cassette to play, he asked while walking back to his seat, 'Could your career be anywhere near law?'

'Not exactly. Why?' I asked curiously.

'You talk like a lawyer in the making. How long would you lock me up to languish in jail if I requested you, in all justice, to be my girlfriend?'

My heart missed one beat, and then another. I just sat there staring at him unable to say anything.

'How old are you now Cathy, if I may ask?'

'Twenty years, four months. And you?'

'Incredible!' He exclaimed, ignoring my question. 'Could anyone be twenty still?'

42

Just then, Frank knocked on the door and finding it was not locked, he walked in.

'What on earth are the two of you up to?' he said, happily shaking Brian's hand.

Frank had grown up to be so jovial and humorous that put together with Father, you would find it difficult to account for the contrasts. Being our first born, he was nearly ten years my senior and I estimated Brian's age to be anywhere near his. He was by then working as a chemist at the Union Carbide. I had found it difficult to resist his invitation to come and stay with him in Nakuru before my exam results were out, so there I was, hardly two weeks after Christmas.

'You didn't tell me you have such a charming sister! I nearly mistook her for your girlfriend. I do not think you are *Frank* after all.' Brian chuckled at his joke.

'I don't *Frank* about my sister. You know she is the only sister I have. I hope you are not applying *Brain* to confuse her.' And they went on joking about their names, oblivious of my presence. In the meantime, I cleared the cups from the table and went to hide in the bedroom.

'How long have you been around?' I overheard Frank ask.

'Over thirty minutes.' Brian must have been consulting his watch for he added, 'Forty seven minutes to be precise.'

'Goodness!' It was Frank this time, 'I have never known you to be this patient.'

Somebody placed a Lingala cassette and I could not overhear them anymore.

It was not until we had taken supper that Brian succeeded in leaving. Frank had insisted, much to my pleasure, that Brian have supper with us. If at all he noticed the intense attraction between us, he never let it show.

I did not see Brian over the two weeks that followed his first visit and I was distracted. Had something gone wrong just when it seemed all right? Had Frank possibly discouraged him from coming again while I was staying with him? Was twenty too young an age for his liking? I tried to gain courage to ask Frank where the hell his friend had vanished to, but my courage failed me. Frank, in turn, went about the house as if the name Brian did not exist in his world. He had made no mention of him ever since the time Brian had left. He was playing *Big Bro* I guess.

The excitement of meeting Brian had not subsided an inch and I could not bring myself to imagine that he would not be mine. There was no end to the castles I built in my mind; the walk down the aisle in a white flowing gown, the vows, the children . . .

Every evening I made a habit of walking to the shops with the pretext of getting one thing or another. Secretly, I hoped to meet Brian. No such thing happened and I gave up the exercise altogether at the end of the third week.

When he finally showed up on the Wednesday of the fourth week I was exasperated. He looked more handsome than I could recall and remarked casually, 'Still around, huh?'

The son of a bitch. Is that all he could say after all I had been through on his account? Even no 'I-missed-you' or, 'You-look-good'!

I let him in though, happy that he was here again. 'What took you so long?' I couldn't conceal the note of anger in my voice.

'You missed me then?' he countered lightly. 'Your bro in?'

'Not yet.' I gave up hope of continuing the attack. 'He comes late on Wednesdays. Mentioned something about playing squash at the club.'

'Damn me to forget. I have watched him several times on Wednesday evenings. He is a good player.'

'You play squash too?' I asked keeping the conversation going.

44

'Not exactly. Squash is actually the middle-class' dream for golf.'

'You play golf then?' I asked sarcastically. After Henry, a man who bragged was the last thing I wanted. He hesitated a while before answering.

'I play no games in as much as I belong to no class. I hate people's obsession of class as though they were living in India.'

I knew nothing about the Indian 'classes' so I changed the topic.

'You have not told me what kept you away for so long.'

'I didn't think you would want to see me again.' He smiled up at me. 'Besides, I have been pretty busy writing up some work report for assessment. You mind a stroll?' He asked at the end of it. I had been prepared for a long monologue on the nature of the report and his work. Didn't men love to talk about their work, especially if the woman was interested in listening?

He said the stroll would not take us far and that we would be back by seven.

I jumped at the suggestion, put on shoes, picked up a jacket and off we went.

To my surprise the stroll ended up at his house. He said it was Freehold estate and that it had no direct commuter transport link with Shabab, where my brother stayed, thus the long walk.

His house was remarkably neat, with everything arranged appealingly.

'It is hard to convince anybody that a woman does not live in here. It is apparently too neat for a man.'

'On the contrary, that is the only person missing in this house.' He disappeared into another room which turned out to be a kitchen. Seconds later he emerged with a tray.

45

'When did you make this?' I asked remembering how long it had taken me to make tea on Brian's first visit. 'You were expecting me then?'

'In a way, yes. Of course I was aware that Frank goes to the club every Wednesday and decided there couldn't have been a better chance to invite you over. Now at least you know where you can find me whenever you wish. I am here most weekdays by six in the evening.' He poured out the tea in both cups and placing one before me said, 'Be my guest, please. And feel at home.' He removed some pamphlets from the coffee table and placed them on a chair beside him.

'Is that the report you have been writing?' I asked sipping my tea.

'No. It couldn't have been typed so fast. These are medical journals I got from a doctor friend. They have kept me busy over the last two days when I wasn't writing. There is this news on the discovery of a new disease. You have heard of AIDS, haven't you?'

I shook my head. There were hundreds of diseases I did not know about. How was I to know of another new one? For your record, Marilyn, note that the year was 1984.

'AIDS is a new disease which has no cure . . .' '*Even cancer has no cure,*' I said to myself. Brian was talking on '. . . was identified about three years ago in America and at the rate it is spreading, people's lives are being threatened.'

'What a name!' I said, dwelling on the trivialities, bidding the topic to change.

'That's just an abbreviation.' Brian explained. Then, consulting the journal, he said: 'In full it stands for Acquired Immune Deficiency Syndrome.'

'Why such a long name? I mean why can't they just give it a simple name like Malaria or Typhoid, sort of a one word name?' I was beginning to like my argument.

46

'Ask the people who baptised it, but I think each of those names help explain its nature.' He searched through the pages of the journal and satisfied, announced, 'Here it is!' Then, reading aloud:

'. . . it says, *Acquired means literally 'to catch' because the disease is caught and not inherited. Immune Deficiency implies 'poor body defence mechanisms against infections' and Syndrome means 'a group of illnessess which help to identify the particular disease', in this case AIDS . . .'*

Then looking up from the journal he commented 'Technical language, eh?'

'How are people catching this – er, AIDS disease? They say there, if I am not wrong, that it is caught.'

This time he replied without consulting the journal. 'They list a number of ways in which the disease can be acquired. One of them is by sexual encounters. Another, through blood transfusions or use of contaminated needles and other materials which can prick. I can't remember the others, but by far the most worrying is that one of sexual intercourse. Americans are being urged to change their lifestyles with regard to sex. The journal notes that if the cure is not found within the decade, then there is fear that there will be an AIDS epidemic in the whole world.'

'What causes the disease?' Our biology teacher had always said that for every problem there is a cause; and for every disease, there is a cause too.

'The causative agent is a virus which they are calling . . .', he searched the journal again. '*The virus is known by the name LAV, in full, Lymphadenopathy Associated Virus. A series of research is still underway concerning the virus.*'

(Marilyn, note that the virus has since been renamed HIV)

'Now enough on AIDS.' Brian said, placing the journals on the side board. 'You can take a copy of that journal if it interests you.'

That is how I came to possess a copy of that journal which I am referring to as I write this letter. I discovered it in a box which had my old letters and magazines.

I pressed on the conversation further. It had turned out to be interesting after all. 'Why are Americans being asked to change their lifestyles? I mean what has that got to do with the disease?'

'Don't you realize that if Americans were to continue with a free-sex lifestyle then they would be encouraging the spread of the disease? They are being discouraged from having many sex partners at a time, having sex with prostitutes and in general avoiding high risk behaviour. The men are being encouraged to use condoms whenever they are having sex with a stranger or an irregular partner.'

'What is so difficult in that?' I asked in a low tone.

'Easier said than done.' Brian said unenthusiastically. 'Take the use of condoms for instance. I must say few men, among my friends that is, would voluntarily choose to use condoms to protect themselves against possible infections. In most instances, they use condoms simply to prevent pregnancy in the woman. One guy in our office amused us by likening the use of condoms to the deduction of income tax from his pay. Another said using the condom during sex is like eating a sweet with its wrapper on. What this suggests is that many people find it cumbersome to use the condom during sex, and with this bias, many of them are likely to be infected or pass on the infection. However, the acceptability of the condom varies from one individual to the next, and it has been found to be generally poor in Africa.'

This Brian wasn't ashamed to mention such things, I remember thinking. I was raised up to believe that any mention of sex was taboo and there was Brian talking frankly to me about sex. Out of embarrassment, I offered no further comment on the issue. We took tea in relative silence, cleared the table and left for home.

On our way back Brian talked of ladies. He said many ladies developed such materialistic tendencies that it was difficult to determine whether they loved a man for what he was or what he had.

'What more do you expect of them?' I countered. 'It appears that in Africa, the economy favours the male species more than the female. You get the best jobs, hold the top positions in any given firm, drive the best cars, own land and everything else. The only way these ladies can get a share of that is through love, fake or otherwise, but rarely through climbing the same career ladder. You men always arrive at the top before them. It's happening in Kenya, isn't it?'

'But aren't you given an equal chance to education? You stand to gain from job opportunities just as much as I do. This is not just a gender issue.'

'You can say that again. The gender issue has not been resolved in Africa when it comes to filling vacancies. Walk into any office. Doesn't it strike you that most lowly positions are occupied by women – the woman receptionist, the woman subordinate, the woman secretary and possibly the woman clerk. On the other hand, most executive positions are occupied by men. Thus the male executive manager, the male financial controller, the male administrative manager – name them. Then you can confidently say that it is not a gender issue.'

'Maybe, the women are not competent enough for the managerial posts. Why else would . . .'

'Have you tried them?' I interrupted, feeling the bile rise. Any discussion on women often had this effect on me.

'Well, I haven't been in a position to. One strong argument is that women often require a break – like the maternity leave – this break is undesirable in the running of a firm, especially if the woman is at the helm.'

'That is the stupid excuse you men give. What I know is that women do not give birth forever. By the age of say, thirty five, most women are through with the procreation business and feel competent enough to challenge men in any capacity. A pity they are never given this chance.'

We waited for a white car to pass before crossing the road.

'I told you, you should have chosen law. Then the women would have a legal representative.' Brian sighed, giving up the argument. I am sure he regretted having started it in the first place.

It was already dark by the time we got to our house. I was relieved to see that Frank had not arrived yet.

'I hope you didn't take that argument personally, Cathy.' Brian said apologetically. 'It is just nice knowing what other people think about certain issues.' He took my hand in his and squeezed it lightly. 'Come on, don't look that upset,' he said again, this time reaching for my lips. We reunited in the long kiss that followed, spiced with the soft murmurs of 'I love you'.

That night I retired to bed feeling pure ecstacy. Could anyone be so happy with life? I replayed the whole evening in slow motion. The stroll . . . the tea . . . the argument . . . Brian's hand squeezing mine . . . then the kiss. I replayed some parts and forwarded others, such as the conversation on AIDS. The idea of the disease threatening lives was so far-fetched, and to imagine that I would be on the victims list within the decade was not even remotely possible. I drifted into sweet sleep thinking of Brian's smiling face.

Chapter Six

Marilyn, reliving the past is like taking an overdose of tranquilizers and drifting into a sleep I would prefer not to be shaken from. How sweet are those memories that end up in Brian's arms! I hate to come back to the present – to the reminder that I am hanging loosely at the end of life.

Speaking of which, I received another of your letters today in which you are cursing and wondering why I am not communicating. What do I write and tell you? That I have changed my mind about going to Texas? That I have tested positive for HIV and cannot be allowed to travel? What would you think, Marilyn? How would you take it? You know the scorn with which people treat the AIDS victims – as though they were suffering from leprosy. All their friends disappear from the scene, and nobody wants to associate himself with the victim, with the exception of a few relatives Have you ever stopped to ask yourself how lonely these people get? Or is it assumed we have had a fair share of company in the past and thus do not deserve it any more?

Don't we still pass for human beings deserving love, attention and company for as long as we still live – or have we degenerated so much as to drop the human status? Please answer me, Marilyn, does one's possession of HIV alter all other facts so that one is considered outcast from one's community of dear friends and relatives? Then why do I feel so neglected and dejected, even before I pronounce that I am an AIDS victim? I am aware a good number of people are not quite bothered, for as long as it is the other person suffering and not them. After all we always imagine lightning striking another house down the street, never our own. Then we can watch from far and offer our sympathies, with never a time coming that we too could be victims. Will the time come when AIDS sufferers will be considered as any other patients with no dejection and desolation? I wonder.

I resumed work yesterday after explaining to the Administration Manager that I would not be going to study this year after all. I said something to the effect that my intake had been approved for the Spring semester and not for the Fall semester as I had anticipated. A white lie, of course. Fortunately, my position had not been filled in so the rest was easy. I have repeated the lie to dozens of fellow workers – ask me how many know when the Fall season or the Spring season starts and ends, and I will tell you none.

'One more thing Catherine,' the Administration Manager had said just when I was standing to leave his office. 'You do not mind a cup of coffee after work to welcome you back?'

There we go again. Does this man care to know that he is talking to a walking corpse? Only that there is no way of knowing.

I smiled back and gave the first excuse on my mind. 'Thanks for the offer, but certainly not today. I have invited some friends over to my house for a cup of tea.' And then noting the disappointment on his face, I added, 'Could Monday be okay with you?'

I saw him consult his desk diary, then without looking up at me he said. 'I have a meeting this coming Monday. I am not sure how long it will take.' Then looking up he suggested, 'Instead of going over the days, why don't you call me up when you are ready?'

'Certainly Sir.' I said with all due respect.

So passing over the infection can be as easy as that? You spot a decent looking beauty, fix a coffee date and probably that's just a beginning, within less than a month of the lunch and coffee dates you end up between the sheets – with one more recruited to the glory of AIDS.

52

I have turned out to be a good observer of evening life nowadays. You know I hardly cook in my house and thus go out most evenings in search of food. Consider these incidents of what a typical evening out can look like for a solo, attractive lady, like myself.

. . . I decide I have been too much indoors and walk out one evening, dressed casually. In the estate I pass by playing children who seem too engrossed in their games to notice the passers-by. Their laughter comes through like an echo resounding from another world. The streets are busy with moving cars and people. I join the stream of people moving towards the town centre, for a brief moment feeling alive and a part of them, breaking out from the cocoon of hopelessness and dejection that is now my house. I quickly decide on which hotel serves the best sausages and break away from the stream, taking the less-crowded route to the Wagon Wheel hotel.

Once there, I choose a seat at the corner where I can watch people almost unnoticed.

The waiter shows up fast enough and I place my order of chips and four sausages. I am feeling very hungry and wish I could even add to the number. But can you imagine somebody across you eating chips and eight sausages? Guess the look I would receive.

Two seats away there is a young couple looking sullen as if they are sharing my sorrows. I cock my ears and in time, 'he conversation falls through.

'The only way out is for you to consider an abortion,' the young man says solemnly.

The girl answers something inaudible at my distance. Her face looks moonstruck.

'Everything is risky, even giving birth,' the boy again, 'I am just too young to be a father,' he adds emotionally, turning to

53

his soda bottle as if for consolation. The girl looks shyly about.

'Anybody occupying this seat?' A husky voice startles me. My eyes look up and rest on a short pitch-black, pot-bellied man with an Export bottle half-filled in one hand, and a glass of the same in the other. He passes to be my father twice over.

Even before I can answer, he places down his beer and makes himself comfortable in a chair opposite mine. I guess in Africa, silence means consent. And to add insult to injury, he removes a packet of cigarettes from his shirt pocket, lights one and puffs the smoke in my direction. And as if that has given him some sort of inspiration, he smiles in my direction revealing a set of false teeth. At this stage I decide enough is enough and after excusing myself I rise up and occupy an empty seat towards the counter. It is Friday evening and many people are pouring in, some with partners, others singly.

Just as I begin to take in the situation, a young, bouncy, jean-trousered guy walks from the counter, shakes my hand as if in recognition, only to let out the century old, 'You look so familiar. Where have we met?' For heavens sake why can't he just say, 'I'd be pleased to make your acquaintance' or something like that? He settles in the seat opposite mine – he is clever enough not to ask.

'I can swear we met somewhere,' he unashamedly presses on with his lie. Another waiter passes by and he calls out, 'Waiter . . . please serve Judith here a drink of her choice.' He then turns to me and enquires, 'What do you take these days?' I dismiss the waiter with a hand gesture. My previous order seems nowhere near so I abandon the idea of supper altogether, hungry as I am.

I stand up gracefully and head for the door, much to the amazement of my young friend. I notice one man wink in my direction and overhear another remark 'nice piece of ass, isn't it'. I am burning with fury by the time I reach the gate. Behind me a car hoots and assuming it is a cautionary hoot, I get out of the way. As I turn to look at the hooting car, I hear the brakes suddenly screech and the car comes to an abrupt halt, a few paces ahead of me. I am quick to notice the driver adjust his side-mirror, probably to view me better? When he is sure I am close enough, he pops out his balding head and asks, 'Care for a lift?'

'Depends on which direction you are taking,' I chip in.

'Well, well . . . let's see. Where are you going?'

'I was just walking to the hotel across,' I lied. Sirikwa is directly opposite, it would sound silly to hike a lift from this position.

'See you there then,' he smiles and sure as hell drives slowly to the Sirikwa hotel. Men are fascinating aren't they? Deciding I have had enough for one evening I walk home – hungry, tired and exasperated.

This is a true account of how I spent one evening in town. Other evenings in town are not markedly different from this.

This evening I did not go to town for supper. I felt I had a lot to write. Just as I was settling down for my supper of scrambled eggs and tea, a loud knock on the door startled me. I have not been receiving visitors of late so I wondered who that could be – Alex?

It turned out to be Cynthia.

'I happened to be in the neighbouring estate and so decided to check if you are around,' she said as she took a seat.

'To say the truth, I did not expect to find you in on a Friday evening. Where is Alex?'

'He called to say he wouldn't be coming this weekend.' I lied.

The truth is, I have not seen or heard from Alex for five weeks to date, ever since that ugly incident I have recorded. Cynthia was a year behind me in Highlands School. She did not manage to make it for 'A' Level but fortunately got admission at Egerton College where she studied Dairy Technology. She works for KCC in Eldoret. On the several occasions we have met, we always seem to have a lot to tell.

'You mind a cup of tea or coffee?' I asked.

'At this time?' It was eight fifteen in the night.

'I prepare my supper very late,' I lied to conceal embarrassment at taking tea and eggs for supper. We talked for a while and the story slowly drifted to sweet gossip.

'You knew Josephine Achieng in my class?' I nodded and she went on.

'She got herself pregnant and has had the misfortune of giving birth to triplets, two boys and one girl.'

'Triplets!' I exclaimed, 'Is she married?'

'That is the joke – she isn't. The man responsible has told her to think twice before pointing a finger at him. He denies responsibility.' We talked about Josephine and other ladies in similar but milder predicaments.

'Wait until you hear this,' Cynthia started all over again, with a tone of enthusiasm this time. 'How could I forget to start with such a hot story. Did you know a certain Kamba girl called Jane? She could have been your yearmate.' She described her a bit, 'Tall and slim, light skinned, good looking, liked to wear her hair in a pony tail? Was among the few ladies suspended for misbehaving during the choir festivals.'

My memory returned at this stage.

'She passed away last month.'

'Oh!' I said curtly. I feel so bad when I learn of the death of such a young person.

56

'Rumour has it that she had AIDS, although she committed suicide.'

My heart somersaulted. 'You can't be serious!' I was truthfully shocked.

'You haven't heard anything yet. Jane was working in Kisumu up to the time she died. Now you know how Kisumu life is – as hot as its weather. Jane liked Kisumu life so much. She was the type who believed in having a good life and to this end she had a chain of menfriends. As the story goes, one weekend she would be dining expensively at the Imperial Hotel, dropped home in a Mercedes, the next she would be in Osiepe Bar drinking humbly with a man intent on spending his last cent on her. She is said to have remarked, quote – *I have painted Kisumu red. There is no pub I haven't been to worth calling itself a pub* – unquote. The same she said, goes for the discotheques.

I sat there dumbfounded, listening to the story unfold. Such are the characters who give AIDS patients and victims a dubious character, unleashing the community's rage on them.

Cynthia went on undeterred.

'I guess sooner or later she discovered that she had contracted AIDS. This did not however slow her down and she continued with her wild lifestyle. When the AIDS symptoms set in, she locked herself up in her house and commited suicide. She was discovered three days later. A suicide note was also found – I have not managed to get wind of what was in it. And along with it was a list of sixty eight names of her alleged sex partners. Where the first name was not given the tribal name was preferred. Some cases had both names given. She did not indicate the period over which she had accumulated the partners.'

Cynthia paused a bit and when I offered no comment she talked on; 'I am meant to understand that she had placed stars against seven names and, like a faithful author of the

57

Jerusalem Bible, she had remembered to put a footnote. It read, quote again - *insisted on using the condom, the lucky beasts* - unquote.'

I considered the news for a brief while, shaking my head and for curiosity's sake asked, 'Who gave you all that information?'

'You won't believe it, I got the news from her sister's friend. I work with her in the same department. She attended the funeral in Machakos.'

Shocking, isn't it Marilyn? Even long after Cynthia had gone I have remained seated on the same chair still horrified with the story. If one girl can deliberately spread the virus this much, how about dozens of others among us who knowingly or without knowing it spread this virus daily? Is there really much hope for mankind? I'll retire to bed at this point with this question on my mind.

*   *   *

Today I woke up late and for lack of something to do, I decided to visit the doctor. I felt there was a lot more I still needed to know about AIDS just to satisfy my curiosity and make me better prepared for any eventuality.

By the time I got there, there was a long queue in the waiting room so I booked an appointment for twelve thirty, two hours away. I passed those two hours in town, window shopping and doing bits of shopping in the process.

When I eventually got back to the clinic, there were three more patients so I joined in the queue. My turn took another eternity to reach.

'Hello Njeri. I haven't seen you for long!' The doctor greeted me happily.

'I've just been around trying to pull myself together.'

'I hope you are managing. And what can I do for you this time?'

'Nothing much.' I said, looking at the littered table. My eyes caught a note book on which the doctor had scribbled. What a handwriting these doctors have! You would think they spent five years in medical school only to learn how best to scribble illegible words.

'I still have a number of things I wish to know. Last time you mentioned something about pre-AIDS conditions. I have been wondering what these are.'

'Oh yes, I assume a lot in most cases, thinking everybody understands my language. Now, I must have mentioned that after the asymptomatic phase some patients progress to pre-AIDS conditions before suffering full-blown AIDS. There are two known pre-AIDS conditions. One is known as PGL, in full, Persistent Generalised Lymphadenopathy.'

He broke off to search for a piece of paper and when he found it, he said 'Good', as he wrote down the words. His handwriting this time was surprisingly neat and clear.

'Lymphadenopathy simply refers to the swelling of lymph glands within the lymphatic system. Now PGL describes a condition which is characterised by a persistent swelling of lymph glands in many places. Persistent in the sense that the swellings may be observed over three weeks or more. Many people with PGL have been found to be relatively well and show no other symptoms except for the swellings commonly in the neck and armpits. A few victims have also complained of fevers or experienced night sweats. That is one pre-AIDS condition. The other condition is known as ARC, which stands for AIDS Related Complex in full.' He paused again to write it down on the pad.

'This condition is very similar to AIDS but the difference is that in ARC, the symptoms are not as severe as in fully expressed AIDS and can easily respond to medication. Here, we observe symptoms such as weight loss, unexplained diarrhoea for say, more than a month, unexplained fevers and night sweats. These symptoms

59

worsen when ARC gives way to AIDS. I hope we are together?'

I nodded, then excusing himself he walked to the door. He must have been checking if there were more patients waiting for I heard him tell the secretary to book in any more patients for the afternoon. I observed him silently remove his white laboratory coat and hang it on a nail on the door.

'Good,' he said again, as was characteristic of him. 'I am now all set for a warm lunch.' Then sitting he said, 'What were we talking about?' He asked this with the authority of a classroom lecturer who had presumably caught his student dozing off.

'I hope I am not inconveniencing you.' I said apologetically.

'No, no. Not at all. I always have enough time for my patients. As a matter of fact, this is the first Saturday lunch I am free enough to share with my wife.' Then, as an afterthought he reached for the phone and dialled a number. When it went through, he informed somebody on the receiving end that he would come home in half an hour.

'Did I answer your question well enough?'

I nodded placing back the paper clips I had been fidgeting over. 'What then are the symptoms of AIDS itself?'

'There are no definite symptoms of AIDS but commonly the symptoms I have given about the pre-AIDS conditions have also been observed among AIDS patients. These are; swollen lymph glands in the neck and armpits, persistent fever or night sweats lasting several weeks, weight loss of more than ten per cent of the body weight in two months or so, persistent diarrhoea, persistent coughing, a profound fatigue persisting for several weeks with no obvious cause. In some patients, oral thrush is observed. This comes as a thick white coating to the tongue and mouth. Skin diseases are also common among AIDS patients. I guess I have listed nearly all the common symptoms attributed to AIDS. Now young lady, I have to get going.'

I again remembered to thank him for his time, to which he replied, 'Any time. Sooner or later you will discover that doctors are one's best friends. We are among the first people to witness a human make his first kicks of life, and often among the last to see him breathe his last. Have a good day.'

We parted at the parking bay as I went on to have my lunch in town, pondering over his last statement.

Chapter Seven

Then we went through that period of intellectual lunacy in the form of university education, but that was not before that dreadful period characterised with drilling and salutations of *afande* ! We were the second pre-university lot to undergo the National Youth Service training before joining the university.

At best, it prepared us for greater lunatic behaviour and military toughness. We checked into the camps soft and fragile and re-emerged militant after the gruesome three months training. The result? We were more organized stone throwers and vehicle stoners than our predecessors who had missed this all important training.

We had learnt to strongly demand our rights. If, by some reason *dialogue (chapati)* was not served as scheduled, there would be a running battle between the students and the authorities, with the Central Catering Unit's (CCU) windows stoned and plates broken in the mess. And we proudly called ourselves students of the highest institution of learning! Looking back, I can only say that we were some bunch of hooligans and lunatics!

The social scene was even more chaotic. I am embarrassed to give an account of what went on in the halls of residence after the majority of students had put down their clipboards. There was the 'box', a ladies' residential hall named after its structural shape. This gave the ladies the famous title of 'boxers'. For their love of hiding in the box, the male students were referred to as cockroaches, or simply as 'roaches'. In my first year I never stopped to wonder why in the lady students' halls of residence, there were almost an equal number of ladies and men after class hours. At the entrance to some halls cars parked outside, varying in their degree of poshness, as outsiders too decided to extend their appetites for women to the university.

The first year boxers were given the university welcome by being paired up pretty quickly within the first two months of reporting.

It was indeed a rare taste of freedom where one did what one wanted, whenever one found it desirable, this time away from the strict surveillance of parents and high school teachers.

The first few days after receiving the student allowance, famously known as 'boom', were the most chaotic. While most ladies utilised every cent they had to beautify themselves and their rooms, a good number of men spent the boom on alcohol, cigarettes and on discos, not necessarily in that order. This was more so for the students who undertook non-professional studies, and in particular, the Bachelor of Arts undergraduates.

There were cases in which some male students brought what they called 'collections' into their rooms. Collections were often prostitutes picked up along the streets in the city centre and paid for their services. In a few isolated cases the collections did spend the night in their rooms and then in the morning, the students would decide they were not paying. If the woman insisted on being paid, she would be kicked out of the room mercilessly and often beaten up.

Recollecting the collective university behaviour is sickening. That is not to say there were no cases of decency. I admired a good number of students who refused to be initiated into the wild behaviour of the mobs. Most of these were in the Christian Union and set out to be as different from the other students as day is from night. This they did as their lady counterparts in the other pool struggled for places in Pumwani maternity wing as if competing to see who would outshine the others in delivering babies. After all it was a free society, wasn't it?

I had been admitted for my first choice and so happily settled for the Bachelor of Commerce degree course at the University of Nairobi's main campus. One line I had not let my parents down on was the academic line, and for this my mother offered incessant prayers to her God.

In turn Marilyn, you went to the Kabete campus for your Bachelor of Science in Agriculture. We visited each other on a number of weekends, didn't we?

After the initial shock of the university culture, I brushed aside the steaming social life and studied fervently. At that time, Brian was still my boyfriend and I made little effort to get involved elsewhere. I saw him almost every fortnight. He would visit the campus on Friday evenings and stay till Sunday afternoon. On a few occasions I travelled to Nakuru to see him.

As misfortune would have it, I discovered I was pregnant at the beginning of my second year of study. At that time (I am not sure about now) the worst thing that could happen to a lady was a pregnancy before marriage. This would invite the wrath of the parents and cause quite a stir in the village community. The AIDS disease had by then started making headlines but it still sounded far-fetched. I never gave it a second thought although Brian still poured over any news on it.

When I finally got the courage to inform Brian, he received the news unshaken. After a lot of discussion we ruled out abortion – or rather Brian ruled it out – and entered the discussion about the possibility of marriage. I was at first elated with the idea of marriage but at the same time realised that marriage would not solve much of the problem. Who would take care of the baby while I studied? Brian? Besides, I was aware that Brian had received admission at Stanford University, California, and had a little less than a year to leave. The more I thought about it the more sick I grew.

About one month after I had broken the news of the pregnancy, Brian urged me to travel home and inform my parents about the possibility of marriage. He said the outcome of this would determine the next step.

I adored Brian for this. He was so unlike Henry in his approach to issues. But then I remembered what my brother Frank had once told me.

'*Do not let your relationship with Brian blow to such proportions,*' he had cautioned when he had discovered we were dating. '*He is a very good fellow, that I know. But remember, too, that he is a Luo and we are Kikuyu.*'

At the time I had wanted to tell him, 'So what? I am not a tribalist. After all my best friend in school was a Luo.' Aren't you Marilyn?

But on this occasion, I started seeing Frank's statement in a new light. My parents were conservative in nature and I knew this too well. I had seen how they had nearly caused disaster when my second brother, Peter, had proposed to marry a girl of the same tribe but from Kiambu district. They gave all sorts of 'odd' reasons and stuck to their guns. Only one thing had saved the marriage – Peter's fanatical determination. There was no stopping him and in the end he married without my parents' blessing. My parents' pride had been badly bruised.

Now here was Catherine, pregnant, and to face her parents with news of marrying from a tribe over which the Kikuyu had developed silent animosity. The two tribes were then undergoing the cold war, akin to that of America and the then USSR.

I decided to give it a try for my love for Brian. Marrying Brian would be a dream come true.

As part of my planned approach, I sent a letter to my mother informing her that I wished to get married as soon as was possible. Brian, I said, wanted the marriage plans completed hastily because he would be travelling to America in less than six months. I conveniently avoided any mention of his ethnic tribe and of the fact that I was pregnant.

I remember informing you of the development, didn't I Marilyn? I needed encouragement more than anything else. Your reply was sharp – 'Do you want to marry a man or the tribe? If I were you, I would choose to marry a man. When will this stupidity of regarding people along tribal lines ever end?' I remember explaining to you that I was not the problem, rather I anticipated that my parents would cause a problem.

Mother wrote back saying it would be better if I were to finish my education first before deciding on marriage. She said Father had read my letter and offered no comment so she did not know what was in his mind. The rest, she said, we would discuss when we met.

I travelled home three weeks from then. Brian had been so anxious to learn the outcome of the visit that I couldn't have postponed it much further. Father was not around that evening so I went ahead to talk to Mother. I relied on her to break the news to Father. We talked briefly about the university and home before my mother opened the discussion that had brought me home.

'You are serious you want to get married?' She had started.

I replied in the affirmative. She mentioned that two of my brothers weren't married, what was the hurry? When I did not reply, she went on to ask me where the man came from. There are some facts you can alter, but this one?

'He comes from Kisumu.' I said feebly, counting the number of pictures on the wall.

Mother stared at me speechlessly. At the end of it she simply said 'I see'.

66

I knew what that meant – I had hit a dead end!

'Is there any particular reason why you feel you should get married to this man?'

I looked at my finger nails, then at the paraffin lamp between us. What was this all about? Why was I here, discussing impossibilities? 'I am pregnant and he is willing to marry me,' I burst out. I knew the truth would come out sooner or later, anyway.

'What embarrassment is this you are bringing to my home, Njeri?' Her tone was sharp and full of anger. She went on, talking of the heathen I was, a let-down, a loose girl and many other accusations I hate to recount.

'And about getting married to a Luo, Njeri, forget it! If only your father would hear of it, both of us would be burnt alive . . . do you hear me? See what happened to Peter . . .,' her voice trailed off. I started to cry.

Marilyn, I will cut the long story short. We have been through it several times and recounting it often depresses me. My parents refused in no uncertain terms to have anything to do with my relationship with Brian. They even refused to meet him on the grounds that he was from the Luo tribe. They fell short of placing a curse on me.

I broke the news to Brian in the softest language possible. He was obviously hurt and at the end of my narration he only said, 'So, that is that'. Whatever that meant. At that instance I knew nothing would be the same again between us. I could not have been nearer the truth.

'There is no use then, you and I.' Brian had said as he made to leave. 'The least you can do for me is to go ahead with the pregnancy and have my baby.'

'Brian please, take it easy. You can't walk . . .' My plea fell on the opening and banging of the door, and with it Brian was shut out of my life.

67

You saw me through that tearful period, Marilyn. You said the sun was sure to shine again on the other end of the horizon after the dark clouds had drifted. Together we cursed the older generation's obsession with tribes despite the willingness of youth to live in a world free of tribal and racial boundaries.

'I will surprise my parents,' you had said, 'by marrying across the race if I get any chance. Then they can hit the roof and bounce back, if they are tennis balls that is.' Now you have the chance, don't you?

I have never forgiven my parents for spoiling the one good thing I had in life. And with this, all hopes of entering the marriage institution went down the drain. 'I cannot always do as they want,' I kept repeating. And even now as I lament my state of victimhood, I still apportion the blame to my parents, for had they allowed me to go ahead and marry Brian, chances are that I would not have met such a tragedy.

I saw very little of Brian over the months that followed and so it was that I received Brian's letter with excitement almost six months later. He was writing from California, said he had been there for thirteen days to the date of his letter. He enquired about our baby. Jimmy for a boy and Whitney for a girl, Brian had written.

The following month I gave birth to a bouncy baby boy. And so Jimmy he was.

Mother, in an extreme gesture of kindness, agreed to take care of baby Jimmy then, as I completed my university education. She has been at it ever since. I visit Jimmy every once in a while at our Murang'a home and he still calls me 'Aunty'.

After Brian walked out of my life, my social life became more reckless. I lost complete control of a strictly moral life

68

because it seemed of no use. It was as if the man at the controls of my life had been shot dead and the vehicle had subsequently lost direction. It was with this feeling, after the birth of baby Jimmy, that I resigned myself to other vices that had not been previously part of my life. That is when I took to the bottle. For days I lived at the bottom of a bottle, seeking answers to the misery that had plagued my life. Before long, I entered into a relationship with Bernard who also had misguided notions about life. Hardly two months later our relationship fell through after I met Morris who was a lawyer in town. I drank less now as Morris encouraged me to concentrate more on my classwork. I was doing my final year then. My affair with Morris was equally short-lived.

Through a classmate, Annette, I met Moses, an elderly man in his late fifties. To call a spade by its name, he was what Kenyans will call a sugar daddy, already married with two wives and children my age. And didn't he have the money to spend on me? The association was what a biologist would call parasitic on my part and exploitative on his part. Since baby Jimmy's birth I had felt a growing need for extra money to cover his numerous needs and mine too. Moses appropriately met this financial end. We shopped at the Sarit Centre, Uchumi, Ebrahims and other big supermarkets. My clothes were straight from boutiques of my choice. This life was good while it lasted.

I completed my university education at about this time and surprised myself with a Second Class Honours, Upper Division. Upon graduation, my parents could not contain their pride. That evening while we were relaxing at a city hotel, Mother revisited the issue of Brian.

'I did not see your friend at the graduation?' She had started. 'Which friend?' I asked for asking's sake.

'Jimmy's father,' she said.

'I thought you had said you never wanted to meet him,' I answered accusingly. 'We are no longer friends. Besides,' I added, 'he is already in America.'

Father looked up from the newspaper. We hardly involved him in our conversations partly because he was always disinterested. He was the kind of male chauvinist who believed nothing good could come out of a woman. Why then the sudden flicker of interest? Had the mention of America done the trick?

'What is he studying?' he asked.

Father asking about Brian? Good heavens.

'I am not sure. All I know is that he is doing his second degree, probably in Agriculture.'

'Does he know about Jimmy?' my mother again.

'I haven't communicated with him since Jimmy's birth.' I lied.

The truth is that I had written to Brian immediately after the baby's birth. He had only sent a card congratulating me on the baby's birth and that was it. He had failed to correspond again despite the flow of my letters to his Stanford address. After a while I had stopped writing too, since I could not keep up with the postal expenses.

'Are you thinking of getting married to him?' Mother continued the dry run questioning.

'You said no and I guess it is just that.'

End of the dry run. Father picked up his paper again and shuffled through its pages, suddenly looking disinterested again. Mother resumed drinking her cup of tea with an expressionless face.

I looked across the hotel and at the same time, a young man seated at the far end smiled at me. I smiled back. He wasn't bad looking, was he? I looked past him to the clock on the wall. It was some minutes to six in the evening. Aunt Alice would be expecting us for the dinner celebration at her place any time from then. I had been staying with her in Buruburu since I had finished my University examinations.

I finished my drink, excused myself and headed for the ladies. My move secured the hoped for result – the young man followed seconds later. We met on the corridor.

'Congrats,' he said looking at my graduation gown.

'Thanks,' I said with a big smile.

'My name is Alex, and yours?'

'Cathy,' I said.

'Those over there are your parents?'

I answered with a nod.

'Here is my card,' he said producing a white gold-printed business card. I could see he worked as a sales representative with IBM.

'Do I expect your call tomorrow morning, say, at eleven?'

'Fine with me.'

'Please, do not forget to phone,' he called to my back as I walked into the ladies.

That is how Alex entered my life – as a graduation package, three years ago. Was this a suicidal move? I wonder. Through his well known connections, he got me this job in Eldoret and we have been lovers since then.

I have seen the better days of my life with Alex. Candle lit dinners, buffet lunches and on some occasions, cocktails. Alex has been gentle and loving, and generous if I may add. He has been paying my house rent, helped furnish my house and occasionally brings me breathtaking gifts. We have been content to have an open relationship, without any mention of marriage. It is impossible to imagine how AIDS got into such tranquility.

But I am no angel. I will be damned if I fail to mention that despite this tranquility, Alex has not been my sole lover. Within these three years, I have had a short lived affair with a university don; spent one weekend out of town with a

71

prominent businessman; had a sexual experience with a gynaecologist and a secret affair with a manager in a leading textile factory here in Eldoret. The big question still remains – who could have passed on the infection to me? All these people are respectable and in dignified positions. Doesn't AIDS care to know about this?

I had written to Brian again after settling into my new job. This time he was good enough to write back. He indicated he had moved in with a white American girlfriend by the name of Denise who was quite crazy about him. They were talking about marriage. That, I guess, partly explained why he had kept me at bay. In a recent letter he mentioned that he had secured a fellowship for his doctorate studies and would not be home for another four years.

We still communicate at a snail-paced frequency, that means only three letters a year from either end. He has been kind enough though, to guide me in applying for a scholarship in American universities.

This letter starts less than four months after I succeeded in winning a scholarship from a Texan University. Little did I know I had already won a place on the list of AIDS victims! And the nightmare continues . . .

Chapter Eight

Amsterdam has a good communication network. There are many electric trains which link it with all the towns within the Netherlands. Virtually every minute, there is a train moving in or out of the central station. And within the city there are numerous buses, trams and underground trains. The underground trains are so swift, they could take you anywhere in the vast city within split seconds. On many occasions, nobody bothers to find out whether you have the ticket or not, so I prefer this means because I travel relatively free. This is risky though. Lots of people board the underground . . .

This paragraph is an excerpt from one of your letters to me which describes your first impressions of Amsterdam. You remember how in the next paragraph you described the social scene, citing the legal brothels of the notorious red light districts, as well as the homosexual bars and sex shops which left you astounded? Gosh! I can draw a pictorial view of Amsterdam without even visiting it, thanks to your vivid descriptions.

I do not know of any underground train system in Kenya, the British colonialists did not introduce such glories here. They found and left us with our smoke-puffing trains. I guess at that time there was no global depletion of the ozone layer to worry about.

As I write, I can't help likening the AIDS infection to the underground trains. I can envisage many people boarding the trains daily from various stations all over the world. Their destinations? These underground trains will take those aboard to their graves, swiftly if I may add.

73

Some people in the world are boarding the AIDS underground trains knowingly by sticking to high risk behaviour and refusing to alter their lifestyles accordingly. Maybe I fit in this category. We knowingly ignore all truths and facts about AIDS, passing by all the warning signals, cheating ourselves that we are enjoying life. In this inferno, we obtain tickets in the form of the AIDS virus and secure ourselves a place on the underground train. Thousands of people are busy obtaining their tickets yearly without giving it much thought, only to realize a shade too late that they must die, to the glory of AIDS.

Some people are passive recipients of the virus. In this category are the unsuspecting spouses, mainly wives, of sexually active men. These too must die for the sins of their spouses, often leaving behind children, rendered orphans, as an AIDS consequence. Soon, we may need to build more children's orphanages than schools as increasingly large numbers of children are being left destitute when both parents perish at the cruel hands of AIDS. What an absurdity!

The AIDS virus seems to be taking advantage of the moral weakness in our society and all other imbalances. Hardly three decades from the time we attained independence, our Kenyan society is morally degenerating, caught at a crossroads between Western behaviour and African morals. You only need to walk in any bar to realise that very few people are taking the AIDS epidemic seriously. A patient observer will see with utter disbelief that most people there are not heeding the AIDS signals. Some men still make passes at any unpaired woman in sight, and in most cases you will see them staggering out in pairs.

I have talked to several men who pick up any woman in sight after gobbling down three or so beers. What makes them behave the way they do? The answers are overwhelmingly similar.

74

'You know Njeri, when a man drinks he just finds himself needing a woman . . . I guess you know that a bird in hand is definitely worth two in the bush.'

I remember the sticker on some buses which says '*I may not be smart, good-looking or rich but I am available,*' is that it?

Another man put it more dramatically; 'You should see . . . after my fifth bottle all the ladies in the bar start to look beautiful. After the seventh they are all angels, looking sweet and decent. I use my sweet tongue and the balance of money in my pocket to hook one of the angels. We end up in a lodging or somewhere with a bed. The next morning, oh Holy shit! How did this ugly woman come to share my room? . . . That's when I begin to think of VD and AIDS.'

Such things do happen, believe me Marilyn. I have heard them from the horses' own mouths. There are AIDS posters, sounding the alarm loud and clear. But if you ask me, they are often in the wrong places. Why can't the Ministry of Health try placing them in pubs, discotheques and lodgings as well? These hide-outs need the message most because here is where much harm is perpetrated.

You have followed the story of my life, no doubt. It does not represent an extreme, out-of-place character by Kenyan standards. It is a fairly normal life for a girl in Kenya. There may be upper and lower cases to it. Yet I have ended up with a place on the AIDS underground train.

My story demonstrates a lot of weaknesses in our society. For one, the lack of appropriate sex education for the growing child. Most parents conveniently avoid informing and discussing with their children matters pertaining to sex and friendship with the opposite sex. They prefer to leave the child in the hands of destiny, hoping that somehow the children will grow up in straightness. This dream comes true for a minority of parents. African parents are now faced with

75

a situation where it will be a must to adequately prepare their children in matters concerning sex as early as is conceivably possible. Teenagers need most guidance and should be informed of AIDS and the consequences of irresponsible sexual behavior. It is best for education to stress abstinence and to give as much information on AIDS in non-threatening terms. This way, many teenagers may be saved from booking a place on the underground train as a result of ignorance.

On a recent tour in Nairobi, while I was trying hard to trace Alex, I observed a pitiable situation which I call 'Who is behind the booming music?' Some of the schoolgirls obviously know the answer. They choose to go to school in the *matatus* with the best music, and you will see them talk to the touts or the drivers, depending on who actually is behind the music. If you are keen enough, you will notice an old twenty shilling note pass to the young girl at the end of the conversation – for chips, I guess. Do the parents of these young girls have even the slightest idea of what goes on when they send their children to school? Sooner or later these young girls join the underground train and life goes on as we bury our youngsters, to the glory of AIDS.

On the wilder side are the young girls who turn to prostitution as a means of earning their livelihood. Nowadays there is no lower age limit to the practitioners of prostitution. I have observed very young girls, as young as fourteen, hanging out in dark alleys or in pubs waiting to sell themselves. Most of the girls in this category dress expensively, will not hesitate to smoke and often drink alcohol like a fish does water. I will not ask why these young girls choose to be prostitutes – the economy is pretty bad. I will not stop to wonder how these girls protect themselves from the HIV infection as well as other sexually transmitted diseases. I guess for those who choose to travel this path, their tickets on the underground train are a guarantee.

Their friends who choose to have affairs with sugar daddies may not be much better placed either. Why do sugar daddies use their wealth to lure young girls? Even after my brief affair with good old Moses I can still afford to ask this question. Could it be that I contracted AIDS from this sugar daddy, who was willing to give me anything money could buy in exchange for my precious life? Those niceties cannot help me now. In a fit of anger I have thrown away all those clothes I was bought by that sugar daddy. A pity I cannot absolve myself from the fact that he used me that way, exploiting my body just because he had the money to. But again I console myself that maybe he is not the one who passed on the infection.

This brings me to my next point. I cannot help but think that AIDS has come to exploit the low status of the woman in African society. Even by the family, the girl is treated as being more lowly than the boy. She is just an investment, a flower that will blossom in spring, yield dowry and wither in autumn. She grows up to be a wife whose rightful place is in the kitchen, with due submission and allegiance to the husband. Girls grow up knowing that they will have to rely on men to provide economic security at all stages of life. From economic dependence on their fathers, they jump right into their menfriends' or husbands' hands. And the men in turn ask a small price for the ladies dependency – the woman's body to fulfil their lust.

A friend of mine recently remarked; 'No matter how much you women struggle for equality, as far as the AIDS infection is concerned, we men still have the upper hand. It is us who wear the condoms'

How right he was, it is the men who choose when to wear the condom and when not to, often with little help from women. And just as so many wives are dependent on men to fulfil their economic and security needs, they are also dependent on the good will of the men not to infect them with AIDS and other venereal diseases. The big question is, how reliable are these men when it comes to not passing the infection on to their wives, when their blood warms at the sight of every beautiful lady in the office or the bar? How many men, on realising that they have contracted a venereal disease, will hesitate to pass the infection on to their wives? You will help me supply the answers Marilyn. But how much worse it is with the AIDS infection, when most people will only realize they are victims when the symptoms come on strong, often several years after they have contracted the virus! I said at the beginning of this letter that the AIDS story is a human tragedy. The web engulfs the innocent citizens as well as those who stick to high risk behaviour. And the future remains oblique as the underground train runs back and forth.

Some people are heeding the alarm signals by changing their sexual behaviour. They have a positive effect on society. However the social concern still remains with the thousands who continue to indulge in high risk behaviour and those who, through ignorance (or is it arrogance) stick to risky cultural practices which have been known to spread the HIV infection. By this I mean practices such as group circumcision, where the circumcision blade is never sterilised between each individual circumcision. I am also talking of practices such as the inheriting of wives by an otherwise healthy man, after the death of a husband possibly from AIDS. This practice is common among Western Kenya tribes.

AIDS also presents a catastrophe to the polygamous nature of African society. I know of a man who had three wives and sixteen children. He contracted the AIDS virus somehow and infected all his three wives. The man died two years ago and has since been followed by two of his wives. I guess the third is still on the underground train, with one foot in the grave. Soon, sixteen children from one home will need an orphanage.

Leave AIDS to the medics, my doctor says. AIDS is a disease alright, but placing it entirely in the hands of the medical authorities is the simplest way of asking the world to commit genocide. We won't have to wait for the explosions of a nuclear war to wipe us out, AIDS is doing the job in a better way. We still await anxiously the good news from the medical researchers to brace us within this century so that the world can receive the wonder drugs and vaccines for prevention. But before then we will have to keep our fingers crossed, guarding our every moment. We are yet to observe radical changes in sexual behaviour among ourselves. The hospital remains the end point; the starting point is what each individual in society does behind closed doors. The AIDS question remains in the hands of every individual to answer. And the underground train still speeds to the hungry world of the dead.

Chapter Nine

As for me, Marilyn, I go about my daily routine in disillusionment, often filled with trepidation and fear. I know I do not need a solution to my problem – there is none. What I need is a miracle as I watch my grace period quickly dwindle. I am like a dry leaf hanging loosely on a tree, waiting to drop down as the wind blows in my direction. I regret every single day I have lived a reckless life, regret every affair I ever indulged in. They say that prevention is better than cure. With regards to the AIDS infection, I will add that prevention is infinitely better than an unknown cure.

When you started to read this letter, I am sure you were shocked to learn that I am an AIDS victim and all through I guess you have been determined to find out how I could have contracted the virus. Now you know how. Do not ask me from whom I contracted the virus. That remains unresolved to me and I guess it will be my new assignment after this letter has reached you.

I have managed to trace Alex and tried to get him to talk. The best he has done was to apologise for manhandling me. I was glad to learn that he is still very healthy and goes about his job energetically. He says he cannot bring himself to go for any AIDS test. It would kill his spirits as well as make him die faster – if he has received the infection that is.

I stayed with him once for four days in Hurlingham estate in Nairobi. All that I have learnt about him was through searching his old letters, his old and recent photographs and from remarks he has carelessly let fall. I was also lucky to receive a phone message from a certain Lucy who left a message that Alex should meet her in the usual place that evening. I had pretended to be Alex's sister over the phone. I was surprised that after three years I did not know Alex well. I am finding it difficult to rule out his being the source of my infection. I still need a lot more information on Alex before I can disclose to you the kind of man my heart has been content enough to have for the last three years. I am horrified at the little information I have in my hands. All that you will find in my next letter. It will be good reading, I guess.

While in Nairobi, I was also fortunate to bump into my lecturer friend. He informed me he was finalising his travel documents in order to go to Britain for further studies. I wonder how far he has gone with this. If he has received clearance, won't that show that he is not HIV positive and rule out his being the source of the infection? I am dying to know if he managed to go out for his studies. The answer might be a useful lead. This evening I will have to walk to Elgon View estate and find out from one of his friends living there if he managed to travel abroad. Again you will get the information in my next letter.

That leaves me with three more suspects, the prominent businessman, the gynecologist, and the manager. I do not know of any approach I could use to find out any information concerning these personalities as the relationships were often short-lived with no notable inclinations towards intimacy. I am sure if I were to bump into the businessman, he would ask 'Where have I seen you?' or 'What is your name again?' I am probably just one of those girls on an endless chain whom he uses every other day to fulfil his lust.

The gynecologist may not have a different approach. He may imagine I am just one of his clients who walks in for an abortion or for a cure for a venereal disease and certainly one who has never shared his bed. One woman once remarked that gynecologists specialise in women's diseases as well as in women's copulation. They never run short of the supply as every face that pops up in their clinics is a female one. How do I start probing such a man's recent and past sexual behaviour?

The manager? Not easy either. Managers are often surrounded by pretty secretaries, clerks and a wide variety of other female employees who would only be too willing to entertain the boss in bed for a few favours – possibly promotions and increases in renumeration packages. And still there are more ladies on the periphery who are willing to sleep with the same manager, hoping that he will fix them up on the list of the employees. These ladies often entertain the manager in vain, with no job forthcoming and possibly only a vacancy on the underground train.

Tell me Marilyn, how do I point out who exactly could have passed on the infection to me? The solution seems ambiguous, as mathematicians would say. The web is too intricate to trace and I am weak, tired and sick of it all.

I am not happy at all, every minute I remember I am on the victims list and that I face a death penalty. Normally when one is building a house and the nail in one hand drops down, he does not stop. Instead he finds another nail and continues to build. However with the AIDS infection, once the nail drops one cannot continue building. You hit a dead end as you do not have much of a future left. You cannot carry on with your dreams. They are still shattered and death looms in the dark. It hurts your pride, takes away your confidences and leaves you with no faith to go by. As if these were not enough, you have to bear the scorn of the society, as it shows little empathy with the patients. Little wonder many such patients opt for a suicidal outlet. These then are my confessions.

I cannot express myself any better than I have done Marilyn. I am also tired of writing as it leaves me exhausted at the end of the day. I need a break to investigate Alex's life before I can embark on my next lengthy letter. Writing has been relaxing in a way; it has also transformed my way of thinking such that I have almost come to terms with the fact that I am an AIDS victim. I still feel shame and regret but I know these will not change. I have good reason to think that if this letter were to be made public after you have gone through it, it would help transform the sexual behaviour of a section of our Kenyan society. I know I will bear the scorn and the stigma but it is the only sane thing to do. Already I have one foot in the grave and another on a banana peel. I will be glad to hear your views after you are through with this letter.

Your sincere friend,

Catherine Njeri.